DOWN AND DIRTY

A J.J. Graves Mystery

By Liliana Hart

ISBN: **1495222551**
ISBN-13: **978-1495222559**

DEDICATION

To Mom:

For always having my back. I love you.

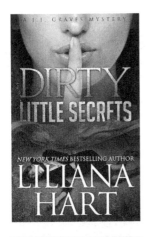
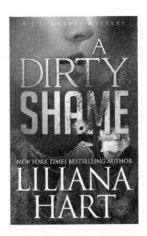

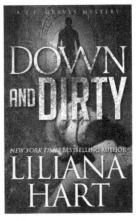

CHECK OUT THE OTHER
BOOKS IN THE J.J. GRAVES
MYSTERY SERIES!

CONTENTS

ACKNOWLEDGMENTS

Thanks to Bryan and Jamey Fontenot for helping me with arson research and having great stories to tell. Any mistakes are mine and mine alone.

Thanks to the team of people who make getting these books out possible. My assistant, Whitney (who makes everything run smoothly), Everything But The Book for organizing everything from formatting to uploading, and to Damon Freeman who makes the best covers ever.

A special thanks to my children and family. I love and appreciate all of you more than you'll know.

And as always, thanks to my readers. I love what I do.

CHAPTER ONE

There was something about a man standing behind a stove that made it hard to concentrate on anything else.

"We're getting married in three days," Jack said.

I rolled my eyes and took a sip of my first cup of coffee, the life starting to flow through my veins and turn on my brain. I wasn't a morning person on my best day, so I'd need at least another pot before I'd be able to talk about the wedding.

I was of the mind that two people in love should just get the deed done with as little fuss as possible. All you had to do was sign your name to a piece of paper and that was that. Pretty anticlimactic when, in my mind, the important part was spending the next fifty years of your life with someone you loved.

I know what you're thinking. That I, Doctor Jericho Jaye Graves—J.J. or Jaye to anyone who doesn't want to get stabbed in the throat with my scalpel—am a pure romantic at heart. But that's pretty much the farthest thing from the truth.

It's not that I don't appreciate romance or know it when I see it, but I'm practical by nature and don't often stop to smell the roses. The good thing is that Jack is almost as romantic as I am, so neither of us feel too bad about talking dead bodies over the dinner table instead of making cow eyes at each other. Though I often think about trying to be more romantic, just to show Jack that loving him really is the first thing I think of when I wake up in the morning and the last thing before I go to sleep at night. And in my mind, thinking is half the battle.

"Don't frown, Jaye. It's bad for your skin." Vaughn Raines had been one of my and Jack's best friends since childhood and had taken it upon himself, along with Jack's mother, to put a wedding of epic proportions together in less than two weeks.

Vaughn owned an antique shop and vitamin supercenter over in King George proper. He dressed like a Wall Street banker six days a week, kept his dark hair and goatee impeccably groomed, and traded in his Mercedes for a new one after Christmas every year. Which in itself made him stick out like a sore thumb.

Bloody Mary, Virginia was as blue collar as it got. So the fact that he was gay went mostly overlooked in a town of more than two thousand busybodies willing to pass out judgment like communion crackers.

I'd noticed a change in Vaughn over the past couple of months, ever since his lover had been brutally murdered. He'd withdrawn and stayed mostly to himself, working longer hours to keep busy. And drinking more to deaden the pain when he wasn't busy. Jack and I had been worried about him, which was one of the reasons I'd given in to having a big wedding in the first place. If it made Vaughn happy to make all the arrangements then I could live with standing up in front of a hundred people to say my vows, even though the thought made my stomach roll.

Vaughn *tssked* and leaned over with the coffee pot to refill my cup. "One day you're going to wake up and look in the mirror and those wrinkles on your forehead are going to be permanent. Then it's nothing but a downward spiral of Botox and tears."

I shot him the finger and heard Jack snicker. "Speaking of Botox, have you guys seen Carla Cassidy lately? I'll hardly have to do any embalming when she dies. A real money saver for the family." My voice broke on the last word and I cleared my throat.

I'd been choked to within an inch of my life some months back and it had done permanent damage to my vocal cords. The mornings were the worst, the words sometimes not coming out at all. But once I warmed up it wasn't so bad. I'd mostly gotten used to sounding like the love child of Kathleen Turner and Lauren Bacall.

"That's just one of the reasons I love you," Jack said. "You're a glass half full kind of girl."

Vaughn put his hand over his heart and sighed dramatically. "The sweetness of your love melts my cynical heart and makes me want to throw up in my mouth all at the same time. You two should get married or something. If Jaye will show up."

"Oh, for God's sake. I have the date and time scheduled in my phone. I even set an alarm just to be safe. I figure if I can remember to bury a body then I can sure as hell remember to get married. Now are you going to feed me breakfast or just torture me with the smell of bacon?"

Vaughn shook his head. "Already the nagging wife—"

"I didn't realize you were going to be such a chicken about getting married," Jack said. "I wouldn't think it'd be a big deal to publicly show that we love each other and want to spend the rest of our lives together. But maybe I was mistaken—" he shrugged and poured eggs into the skillet.

I scowled. "Low blow, Sheriff. You know I want nothing more. And I do love you."

"She's got stage fright," Vaughn said. "Remember when she was Pilgrim Mary in the Thanksgiving play in third grade? Just one line. That's all she had to say."

I glared at Vaughn, but it didn't do any good. Jack's body was shaking with laughter and he used the cup towel tucked into the waistband of his sweatpants to wipe at his eyes.

"If you want to live you'll stop talking," I growled between my teeth.

"Ooh, I'm terrified," Vaughn grinned. He turned back to Jack. "For as long as I live I will never forget the look on Melanie Rose's face after Jaye threw up on her. Priceless."

Jack winked at me and went to get the

bacon out of the oven. "Jaye's always been good at making friends. Is Melanie on the guest list for the wedding?"

"You're a riot, Jack Lawson. It took twenty years for Melanie to stop going the opposite direction when she saw me on the street. If I were you I'd be more worried about a repeat of Melanie Rose all over your tuxedo. There's still time for us to fly to Vegas and let Elvis marry us."

"I'll take my chances. If you start looking a little green I've decided to give you a quick pop in the jaw and knock you out. Reverend Thomas is mostly deaf anyway, so he'll believe me if I tell him you said I Do before you pass out."

"And here I am still waiting for bacon. The abuse I take from you two is unbelievable."

"Woman, you've got your coffee and you've still got razor burn on your neck from this morning. Bacon is just icing on the cake."

I felt the heat rush to my cheeks and fought the urge to touch my neck. I decided the safest thing for me to do was finish my coffee.

"And don't think I haven't noticed how you're trying to change the subject about the wedding," Jack said, putting eggs, bacon and hot biscuits on three plates and bringing them over to the breakfast nook.

I blew a raspberry at him and decided not to comment. Instead I took a moment to appreciate the vision he made. I was lucky to have him in my life, and I was grateful for it every day. He'd saved me—both mentally and physically—and I knew there was no one else I'd ever be able to count on or trust like I could him. I still wondered what he saw in me—why he loved me. Though it didn't occupy as much of my thoughts as it once had.

Don't get me wrong. Jack was something spectacular to look at, but it wasn't why I loved him. His looks were just part of the package—dark hair cut close to the scalp and threaded with the occasional strand of silver. His eyes were the color of dark chocolate and went almost black when he was aroused or angry. His body was sculpted by years of physical fitness he'd had to maintain for the job. But that wasn't the only thing that told the story of his life as a cop. The scars on his right side caused by three bullets that he'd gotten from a SWAT raid gone wrong were puckered, and a stark reminder of the life of service he'd chosen.

Jack was a man whose integrity and moral code would always stand up under any scrutiny. A man I could be proud of and respect. And it tore at my heart to see the pain the job had caused over the years—a job people took for granted—filled with danger and deeds that wore on the soul and the psyche.

I'd never given much thought to what it meant to be a cop's wife. Or anyone's wife for that matter. Dealing with the dead on a daily basis wasn't always conducive to a healthy relationship. Neither was having felons for parents, or a father who'd decided to come back from the dead and who might be a murderer.

Jack seemed to think I was overanalyzing things and had decided to love me anyway. But I worried about what would happen the day Jack had to arrest my father and send him to prison where he belonged. Or worse, if Jack had to pull the trigger and take him out. I didn't want to believe my father was capable of violence, but I'd seen the evidence in a body buried in a secret bunker that only my parents knew about.

"Jaye," Jack said, sitting across from me. He took my hand and squeezed it once. "You're thinking too hard. Everything is going to be all right."

I nodded and tried to smile, but I'm not

sure I pulled it off. I loved Jack with all my heart and soul. He was the one constant in my life, and despite my fear of the wedding, I'd walk through hell or high water to say those vows in three days. And then I'd wait for the other shoe to drop. Because I'd learned that life was a fickle bitch.

A cell phone rang and all three of us scrambled to see whose it was. Jack reached his phone first and held it up to show he was the one ringing.

"Sheriff Lawson."

I knew it was work related by the way his face lost all expression. Jack was one hell of a poker player. He turned and went over to the sink, standing with his back to us as he continued the call.

"How was the final dress fitting?" Vaughn asked.

I focused on cutting my biscuit in half so I could pile on the eggs and bacon to make a sandwich, ignoring Vaughn's question as a pang of guilt hit me.

"Seriously, Jaye? You missed your appointment?"

The look he gave me was not a good one, and I shrugged and mouthed sorry as he got out his phone and dialed. I'd meant to go to the final fitting for the dress. At least that's what I'd say if anyone asked. But in all honesty I'd forgotten about it, despite the numerous reminders I'd had posted everywhere.

It hadn't been a quiet week for death. The bad news was that five families had said goodbye to loved ones over the last several days. Not great odds considering King George County wasn't overpopulated to begin with. The good news was that death paid the bills. And I had a lot of bills to pay, including years of student loans from med school and debts that my parents owed after all their assets had been seized—except for the house and the funeral home because they'd had the foresight to put them both in my name.

"Three o'clock today," Vaughn said, hanging up. "I will meet you at the funeral home to pick you up at two-thirty. Be there or I'm going to tell Clover Dawson you've been meaning to come by and pick up one of her ovulation potions, but you're too embarrassed to ask."

"That's just mean," I grumbled. "I'll go try on the dress. I just don't want to look stupid. Everyone is going to be staring at me."

"You're the bride, you dumbass. People are going to look at you."

"You guys know I'll be there, right?" I

asked, hoping the men in my life didn't really think it was possible I'd be a no show for my own wedding. There was nothing that could keep me from marrying Jack. Not my fear of standing in front of all those judgmental people, or my father showing up out of the blue to walk me down the aisle in front of a room full of cops, just for shits and giggles. I wouldn't put it past him. He was perverse like that.

Vaughn winked at me just as I heard Jack say, "We're on our way."

"Well, that's never a good sign," I said with a sigh. I quickly made a breakfast sandwich for Jack and wrapped it up in a napkin.

He hung up and I could see the news on his face—that it was going to be bad.

"Let's roll," he said, heading toward the stairs to our bedroom to change clothes. It must have been really bad for him not to look me directly in the eye.

"I'll take care of things here," Vaughn called out behind us. "Jaye, wedding dress! Three o'clock."

"Stop nagging. Thank God I'm not marrying you."

"I've often felt the same way. Your vagina is a deal breaker."

I burst out into laughter. I could always

count on Vaughn to lighten my mood. I had a feeling it would be the last time I felt that way for a while.

CHAPTER TWO

"I take it I'm following you to the scene?" I asked, just to break the silence. Jack hadn't said anything or told me the situation, which was unusual in itself.

"EMS is on scene and they'll transport. The number of bodies hasn't been determined yet."

He pulled on jeans and a white undershirt and then topped it with a long sleeved flannel shirt in shades of dark green and blue. The mornings were still cool, even though we were well into spring, but the afternoons could get pretty warm, so layering was usually the best bet. He strapped on his ankle holster and slipped his knife into his boot. And then he put on his sidearm and hooked his badge to his belt.

Watching him get dressed every morning always fascinated me. It was efficiency in motion—muscle memory from years on the job—though Jack hardly needed the weapons he strapped on every day to be dangerous.

I pulled on my own jeans, t-shirt, and flannel and then ran a brush through my hair. It hung just past my chin and pretty much did the same thing no matter how I styled it. I probably needed a trim, but I had a tendency to forget things like that. My hair was straight and black. It'd never be anything else.

I never bothered with makeup unless I had to. I'd gotten in the habit of doing without it over the years. Through medical school I was always too tired to bother, and I'd found that the dead didn't really give a shit what I looked like. I was fortunate in that I had good skin and excellent cheekbones, which I'm assuming I inherited from the biological French mother my parents stole me from. My eyes were gray—like fog—with no other blue or green color variations that came out when I wore certain colors. Just gray. And my lashes were dark and thick and naturally lined, so putting on eye makeup was overkill for the most part.

It was also a nice bonus that Jack seemed

to find me most attractive in my natural state. I was never sure if he was just saying that to be nice or if he really meant it, but I was leaning toward the idea that he was being genuine. Jack and I hadn't been having sex for all that long, but I'd found I needed to take my vitamins on a regular basis to keep up. Vigorous was the best word I could think of to describe Jack when sex was involved.

"I'm tight on space in my morgue. I've got Chloe Sanders and Bernie Harrison on ice until their interment. I was going to embalm them both today, so that will make some room, but it'll be a few hours before I have the space available. If there are too many bodies you might want to send a couple of them outside the county."

"It's a family, so it's best to keep them together."

"Oh, man," I said, feeling my stomach sink. No wonder he'd been so somber. "Kids too?"

"At least one that first responders know of. They're from King George so we want to keep it local."

I grabbed my bag and made sure my camera was inside, and then we headed down the front stairs. I heard Vaughn in the kitchen stacking dishes, but he was talking on the phone so we didn't tell him goodbye.

The sun hit us in the face and I slipped on my sunglasses. It was one of those cloudless days where the brightness hurt the skin and the air was so crisp and clear the lungs burned after the first inhale of fresh air.

I used a black extended size Suburban that had been modified for my needs instead of a hearse to haul bodies. I could fit two in a pinch, but any more than that required multiple trips, so I was glad EMS was on the scene.

I went to the back of my Suburban and grabbed my coveralls and slip on rubber boots that came up to the knee. Neither was attractive, but I'd learned from experience to be prepared for anything. Death was often messy.

"Are you going to fill me in on the scene or make me play twenty questions?"

Jack put his cruiser in reverse and backed down the driveway. Then he looked down at his watch. "Fourteen minutes. I'm surprised you lasted that long."

"Dude, that's not cool." I smacked him on the shoulder and he smiled.

"I've got to find my entertainment where I can get it with this job."

The smile vanished and his eyes grew distant. It was a look I recognized and knew to never pursue with questions. There were things that haunted Jack. Things that had happened on the job he'd never shared and that I'd never ask about. But it would take a blind man to not see the pain and burdens he carried.

He cleared his throat and turned onto Queen Mary to head into town. St. Paul's Episcopal church sat on the corner and Reverend Thomas was in the parking lot, directing the gardeners like a drill sergeant on where to plant the petunias. Jack beeped the horn and we both waved.

Reverend Thomas waved back, but his lips were pursed in a disapproving line. He was a nice man and had always been kind to me, but he was also an old school Episcopalian preacher, and the fact that Jack and I were living in sin together before marriage was a point of contention. There'd been a moment I'd worried whether or not he'd perform the wedding ceremony on Saturday, but to my knowledge he was still going to show up.

Trees were green and bursting with new leaves and canopied over the two-lane road. The houses on Queen Mary Road were older for the most part, box-style and wood framed, built during the 1940's. The occasional American flag waved from a flag holder attached to the houses and lawns were neat and freshly mowed. Sidewalks were cracked and uneven with age and neighbors knew each other's names.

I'd heard people say that driving through Bloody Mary was like looking at a snap shot of good old-fashioned Americana. A Norman Rockwell painting that was good at disguising the darker sides of life—the domestic violence that increased during the winter months or the meth labs that popped up from time to time back in the forested areas. Sometimes ignorance was bliss.

I did always enjoy driving down Queen Mary though. Something about it filled me with nostalgia—memories of sitting in the back of my parents' station wagon and driving down the same street on the way to church or school—and it was nice to pretend that for the time it took to drive the length of the street that everything was perfect.

It also made me grateful that I lived far outside of town, because I couldn't imagine being so close to neighbors that they were familiar with what time your coffee kicked in and the subsequent bathroom trip.

There wasn't a fast way to get from our house to anywhere in Bloody Mary, and at eight o'clock on a weekday morning with school and work traffic, things were crawling at a snail's pace. It would be another half hour at least before we made it to the scene.

"You know the Marcello House?" Jack asked.

"Is that the big estate out past the state park on 218? The one that looks like a mini White House but draped in wedding cake icing?"

"That's the one," he said. "Oh, for Christ's sake. Would you look at that?"

I recognized the blue Cadillac and shook my head in disbelief. Mrs. Meador was at least a hundred years old and shouldn't be allowed behind the wheel of a car. Every morning like clockwork, she and three other ladies, whose combined age was almost as old as Bloody Mary, met for coffee. They sat at the window table so they could look out onto the street and gossip about the people in town. Mrs. Meador had once told Jack that when you reached a certain age laws were more guidelines than something that had to be obeyed.

It didn't do any good to write her citations because she never paid them. And putting a warrant out for her arrest would only be a pain in the ass when Jack had to run for reelection for sheriff. It wouldn't look good to lock up a little old lady behind bars and have her family—which was a good portion of the people in town—coming to visit every Sunday after church.

Jack got on the phone and scrolled through his contacts. "Kristi, this is Jack. Mrs. Meador is parked on the median again where Queen Mary and the Towne Square intersect. Tell her she needs to move it or it'll be towed."

Kristi Chen was the newest of Jack's officers, but she wasn't by any means a rookie. She'd come from Atlanta PD about a month ago after she'd had to wade through the carnage of the Greenwood Elementary School shooting. She'd tried turning in her badge, but her chief had recognized a good cop when he saw her and convinced her to get some distance and take another job. Chen had been fine with taking a pay cut and a slower pace of life in exchange for peace of mind. Though I'm not sure living through an experience like that would ever bring peace of mind.

Kristi must have said something amusing because Jack snorted out a laugh and said, "Better you than me," and then he hung up.

We waved at a few of the parents in the school line and several store owners who were opening up for the morning. Once we turned onto 218, Jack pressed the pedal to the floor and we flew down the highway.

"Anyway, I was saying before I got distracted, the Marcello House was bought several years back by the Connelli family. The house is almost a hundred and fifty years old, and they got it for a steal because it had been left vacant more than forty years and needed a lot of renovation. But they bought as is and moved in immediately with the walls crumbling around their ears from what I understand. We're checking into the reasons behind that."

"It's a beautiful house. At Christmas the papers always advertise it as part of the historical tour."

"They did a couple of million dollars worth of renovations, and it took two years to complete."

"I'd rather stick needles in my eyes than deal with all of that construction for two years."

I'd grown up in a three-story Victorian at the opposite end of the same street where Jack and I now lived. It had been a white elephant of a house and every time I turned around something else was wrong with it. It had also been a convenient location for my parents to secretly transport bodies by boat because the Potomac butted up to the back of the property. Needless to say, it was on the market. I'd thought briefly about burning it to the ground just to cleanse the memories, but Jack convinced me the jail time would be an inconvenience.

I'd gotten used to Jack's driving over the years, so I didn't flinch when a tractor pulled out into the road from one of the fields. Jack swerved into the oncoming traffic lane to pass him and then jerked the car back in front of the tractor to cut him off. Nothing pissed Jack off more than when someone deliberately pulled out in front of him and then slowed to a crawl.

My pulse hardly sped up at all and my pants were still dry. "I take it the family who bought the house are the ones who will shortly be occupying my morgue space?"

"That's what it looks like, but you'll need to verify. There was a house fire last night. And because of the age of the house it went up like a matchbox. The fire department responded just after midnight, but the whole thing was so far gone there was no hope of going in to look for survivors.

"They put out the fire and then had to wait until first light to start going through the premises. KGFD discovered two bodies on the search, which officially made it a crime scene until we can determine the cause of death. FD called us, and Detective Lewis responded to the call since he was on shift. It took a little time to track down a judge to get a warrant to enter the premises, but he's got it and is on the scene now."

"Warrant?"

"We still have to get a warrant to investigate the property. It's a private residence. And all fire related deaths are treated as homicides until cause of death and the origin of the fire is determined."

"I knew that about the fire related deaths, but didn't realize you needed a warrant when there was nothing left of the house and no survivors. The law…it's a quandary. Who'd have thunk it?"

"People that pay attention?" Jack asked, arching a brow. "Which is apparently not you. Or Mrs. Meador."

Considering up until a couple of months ago I was buying my birth control pills out of the back of Leroy Brown's trunk, I decided it was probably best not to continue this line of conversation. A girl has to watch her pennies where she can.

Most of Highway 218 was two-lanes of hills and curves through forested areas. Most of the left side of the street belonged to

Caledon State Park, but just past that the land opened up to private residences.

The houses were few and far between and sat far back from the road, including the Marcello House. Or what had once been the Marcello House. Jack turned his unit into a long driveway, the black wrought iron gates propped open to allow easy entry and exit for all the first responder vehicles going in and out.

Despite the fact that we were coming onto the scene rather late, there was still a contingency of fire trucks, ambulances, and cop cars.

Jack hadn't been kidding about what the fire had done to the house. What had once been two stories of antebellum estate—white columns, wraparound porches, and an exterior staircase leading to the massive front doors that had been a work of art—was nothing more than blackened rubble.

The brick chimneys that had been at each end of the house still stood, but the center of the house had been gutted, the upper stories collapsing onto the lower. Large holes where walls had once been yawned into a cavern of darkness, still smoking with the remnants of the fire.

You didn't realize how many materials were

used to build a house until you saw it as rubble—wood, glass, insulation, bricks, ceramic tiles, toilets, and hearths—littered through the remains of the house with no rhyme or reason, but placed at the monster's whim.

I let out a breath and started preparing myself mentally for the scene. It was easy in our line of work to lose our humanity. To become hardened to the atrocities we saw on a day to day basis. But the only way to survive those atrocities was to not think of the bodies as anything other than the job. To not imagine them with expressive faces or going about their day to day lives.

"I hate it when it's kids."

Jack looked at me with his brows raised in question, worry in his gaze. I hardly ever talked about the parts of the job that bothered me. I buried it. Just like he did. It was like an unspoken code of honor between those who worked scenes like this. You made jokes or played it off as inconsequential. But you never talked about it. About how the images stayed in your mind forever and haunted your dreams, catching you off guard at random moments throughout the day and bringing you to your knees with the horrors of it all.

"Sorry," I said, before he could ask if I was

all right. "I think marriage is making me soft. Let's get this done. I've got an appointment I can't miss at three."

He squeezed my hand once and we got out of the car. I pulled on my dark blue coveralls and zipped them up. Jack had his own gear and was already suited up by the time I finished pulling on my boots. I pulled my hair back into a stubby ponytail, and then dug in my bag for a pair of gloves.

I'd started wearing the engagement ring Jack had gotten me on a chain around my neck because of instances like this. I was terrified I was going to lose the ring taking it on and off at scenes. It had been in Jack's family for a long time, and I didn't want to be the Lawson bride who lost part of the family fortune by dropping it inside a chest cavity or losing it at a crime scene.

I saw Detective Lewis heading in our direction from the corner of my eye and groaned at the sight of the man who accompanied him.

"Oh, damn. I guess it was too much to hope that anyone but him would be here."

"He's the fire chief. Who were you expecting?"

Larry Edwards had been the fire chief for King George County for as long as I could remember. He was a couple of inches taller than my own five foot eight and in good shape for a man who had to be approaching sixty. His hair was solid silver and he wore it in the same crew cut he'd had since his days in the military. I was pretty sure I'd never seen Chief Edwards in anything other than the uniform of black pants and white shirt with the fire department emblem on the sleeve.

Larry and my dad had been rivals growing up in Bloody Mary, and it had extended into adulthood. So when my mom and dad were suspected of driving over a cliff in a murder/suicide, you could say that Chief Edwards wasn't exactly broken up by the news. And when the FBI had started sniffing around shortly after to investigate the smuggling ring that had been running through Graves Funeral Home, Edwards had been downright gleeful.

The malice he had toward my parents extended to me as well. Not because I'd done anything to earn it. At least not to my knowledge. I guess I was just lucky. Sins of the father and all that nonsense.

"Well, I'd prefer someone who didn't look at me like they were wishing I'd drop dead at their feet."

"Look on the bright side, babe. At least

Floyd Parker isn't here."

I groaned and shot Jack a dirty look. If I made a list of past mistakes, Floyd Parker would be item number one. Don't get me wrong. Floyd was a good looking guy. He had a Clark Kent kind of vibe going for him. And he was smart. So one would think he'd be right up my alley as far as passable man traits go.

The problem with Floyd—one of many— was that he was basically a douchebag. He would have sold his own mother to the Devil if it meant getting the break on a story or furthering his career.

He'd been a few years older than me in school, and we'd never run in the same circles, but I'd always heard gossip from the older girls that he was excellent in bed, and there was a very convincing poem written on one of the bathroom stalls at the stadium that proclaimed the same.

Medical school was a lonely existence. That's my only excuse. I'd run into Floyd one night while I was picking up Chinese takeout and somehow ended up bringing him back to my place for the night. The Chinese food was delicious, but I'd been disappointed that the sex hadn't lived up to the poem. In fact, it had been awful, but I considered the possibility it might just be me and the fact I hadn't had a full night's sleep since I started med school.

Floyd had been a general dick about the entire experience and had stopped up my toilet just for good measure before he snuck out the next morning. I pretty much put the whole thing out of my mind until a year and a half ago when my parents drove over that cliff. Floyd had been the first to suggest that it had been a murder/suicide, claiming that witnesses had seen them fighting.

I already wanted to kneecap him just for clogging my toilet and being awful at sex, but messing with my family made me want to shove my embalming wand where the sun didn't shine and turn it on full blast. Needless to say, I stayed out of his way unless I couldn't avoid it. Things would be awkward for Jack around reelection time if he had to give me conjugal visits in jail.

"Twenty bucks says he'll be here before we leave the scene," I said.

"That's a sucker's bet. Fifty he's here in the next ten minutes."

"You're on. Will you spot me a fifty?"

Jack laughed and squeezed the back of my neck, giving me all the support and courage I needed to deal with what I was about to face—the victims—not the assholes who crossed my path from time to time. I was used to that.

I slung my bag across my torso and we went to meet Edwards and Lewis half way.

"Sheriff," Detective Lewis said, nodding at Jack. "Hey, Doc." He gave me a knuckle bump and a slap on the arm.

Lewis was a good guy. Like Chen, he'd moved from being a cop in the big city—in his case, Chicago—to a slower pace of life. I had no clue what Lewis's story was or what had brought him here, and I knew enough about cops to not ask unless they volunteered the information.

I grinned and looked Lewis over from head to toe. He was city slick and wore pressed slacks and a white dress shirt, his patterned blue tie knotted crisply at his throat. He'd at least had the presence of mind to put on boots, but they were expensive and made of suede, and already they were wet and blackened with soot.

"Nice boots," I said.

"I've got an image to maintain, Doc. I'm hoping Chen will take notice of my keen sense of style and agree to go out with me one of these days."

"How many times have you asked her?" Jack asked.

"Just four. But I'm starting to make some headway. She's one of those women that never says yes on the first try."

I shook my head in disbelief. Sometimes it amazed me that men were able to find a woman at all with the thoughts—or lack thereof—that went through their minds.

"She'd probably take more notice if you started calling her by her first name instead of treating her like one of the guys. You shouldn't treat a woman you want to impress like you do Martinez."

Martinez and Lewis worked as partners from time to time, and they were good friends off shift. But as with most cops, their conversations often had the maturity level of a twelve year old.

"You think that's what I'm doing wrong?" he asked, tugging at the knot of his tie to loosen it a bit.

"One of many things," Jack said. "The most prevalent being that you're not that big bruiser of a boyfriend she has. That man would break you in two if he caught you sniffing around her."

Chief Edwards snorted out a laugh and shook his head. "Sorry to ruin your morning Sheriff, but I'm glad you came out." He held out his hand and he and Jack went through the typical greeting ritual that had to transpire before any business could be conducted. Edwards ignored me completely.

"Any problems getting the warrant?" Jack asked Lewis.

"Other than pulling the judge off the golf course and ruining his game?" Lewis asked. "Other than that, no issues. Martinez and I have been inside with the arson guy."

"Is arson suspected?" I asked.

"Nothing obvious so far. Arson guy thinks he's found the source, but he's got to run some tests. Could be an electrical malfunction. We marked all the bodies for you nice and neat, which is why my three hundred dollar shoes are ruined."

"Just don't send me the bill," I said. "Serves you right."

"Boy, you're a cop," Edwards said. "No cop I know of wears three hundred dollar shoes. You on the take?"

Lewis flushed red and squared off his stance to face Edwards directly. He looked like a bantam rooster ready to attack. Lewis had a reputation for his temper being quick on the trigger, which is why everyone went out of their way to rile him up. Cops were perverse like that.

I bit the inside of my cheek to keep from

laughing. I was mostly just glad Edwards hadn't been outright hostile the moment he'd seen me. I could deal with being ignored.

Footsteps came from behind me and I moved closer to Jack to widen the circle a little. Detective Martinez stepped up and slapped Lewis on the shoulder with affection.

"Nah, Lewis isn't on the take. His mama sent him those boots for his birthday. He *loves* his mama." Martinez made kissy face noises and Lewis elbowed him in the gut.

Martinez was Lewis's opposite in almost every way. Dark skin, dark eyes, and dark hair. He'd spent some time in the Army and had only been a cop for a couple of years—not long enough for the shiny idealism to have rubbed away—but long enough to develop a cocky attitude and camaraderie with the guys.

I'd gotten used to cop humor over the years. Especially at a particularly difficult scene. The inappropriate jokes and comments were just par for the course. A way to cope. We'd all learned it was better to laugh, the only alternative was to start crying. And once you started crying there was the very real possibility that it would open a whole host of emotions that were better left buried.

"You get a new arson investigator?" Jack asked Chief Edwards, getting things back on track.

"Sure did. Fire is big business nowadays. Lots of rich folk are buying up industrial property in the county, thinking we're too stupid to figure it out when it burns to the ground within a week or two of purchase. People are idiots."

"We'd all be out of jobs if they weren't."

"True enough." Chief Edwards pulled a pack of cigarettes from his breast pocket and tapped the bottom three times before removing one to stick between his lips.

I'd always been fascinated by how people who smoked were able to talk around a cigarette hanging out of their mouth. It was almost hypnotizing, the way it bobbed up and down, the mouth not opening to form coherent words.

"New arson guy is from Arlington. Worked at PD undercover a decade and then transferred to homicide until he made his twenty-five last month and retired. He said he was bored with retirement after the first forty-eight hours, so I hired him. And he's a damned thorough investigator. Relocated to your neck of the woods, Jack."

"Oh, yeah? He must be the mystery man I keep hearing about around town. Speculation is he's a kidnapper or running drugs because of the strange hours he keeps. How he's managed to sneak in and out of his house without being seen is anyone's guess, because believe me, his house is the most watched in the neighborhood. The women on that street consider it their duty to stay well informed."

"Thank God for 'em. I wouldn't know half as much as I do if it weren't for the busybodies in this county." Edwards finally lit his cigarette and took in a deep puff, exhaling long and slow in my general direction. I didn't give him the satisfaction of coughing, but just turned my head to suck in fresh air.

Edwards nodded toward the wreckage of the house and said, "There he is now."

A man in a black Nomex jumpsuit and heavy boots made his way carefully through the debris, his hard hat low over his face so I couldn't see his features. He held a clipboard horizontally and occasionally made notes or sketches.

"Walker," Edwards called out.

"Oh, damn," I whispered soft enough that no one else heard me. There'd been something about the way he carried himself that sparked recognition, but I didn't place it until his name was mentioned.

I appreciated the fact that Cal Walker wasn't someone to be called to heel. He'd always been his own man, forging his own path. He acknowledged Edwards with a head nod, but didn't rush over to greet us. He finished what he was doing and then stepped up over the threshold and off the concrete slab, kicking his boots against the sidewalk a couple of times before heading in our direction.

I could tell the moment he recognized me. He tipped his hard hat back and his face broke into a grin. Cal had been a good friend back in my ER days—more than a friend. He was just one of those guys who was liked by everyone. Laid back and ready for a good time, with a quick sense of humor and ready smile. He was a cowboy, pretty much doing whatever the hell he wanted and bucking the rules if he thought his way was better. He'd never married and had had no plans to settle down, at least back when the two of us were seeing each other.

Cal had been the one serious relationship that had lasted a significant amount of time before Jack. But we both knew early on it would never lead to anything. Cal didn't want long-term commitment, and I couldn't devote enough attention to a relationship with the hectic hours I was working at the hospital. So we'd said our goodbyes and parted as friends.

And we hadn't seen each other since.

"Doctor Graves," he said, the grin still on his face. "Damn, it's good to see you. What's it been? Five years?"

"Pretty close."

I couldn't help but return the smile. Cal was just a *nice* guy. He leaned in and gave me a big bear hug, picking me up off the ground. I usually tried to maintain a professional façade whenever I was out on a scene, but he was making that difficult. I could feel Jack's eyes on me, but I'd somehow lost the ability to speak. Or at least talk my way out of this one.

"Woman, you haven't changed a bit. Still as beautiful as ever."

I was pretty much thinking the same thing about him—a man a little over six feet tall, dark blond hair in need of a trim, a couple of days worth of stubble on his face, and pale green eyes that were full of good humor and framed by laugh lines that women cursed, but that always seemed to make a man look more distinguished.

I'd met Cal my first year out of medical school while I'd been working the night rotation at the hospital. He'd come in after wrestling with a dealer hopped up on coke who had a knife the size of my forearm. The dealer ended up in the morgue and Cal's arm had been sliced from shoulder to wrist all the way to the bone.

I'm not sure how he talked me into it, but I'd agreed to go out with him by the time I finished stitching him up. He was fifteen years older than me, and I hadn't given a damn. He'd been charming, even while in pain, and our personalities had clicked immediately. My relationship with Cal had been the flash and burn you always hear about, but it was impossible for that heat to sustain itself over a long period of time.

Cal squeezed me once more and sat me down, and then backed up a bit so he could see the whole group. Everyone had varying looks on their faces. Chief Edwards was annoyed, Lewis kept glancing at Jack, Martinez was trying not to laugh, and Jack— let's just say Jack's thoughts were unreadable at the moment.

I finally got my wits about me after the surprise of seeing Cal and moved closer to Jack.

"Cal Walker," he said, extending a hand in Jack's direction.

"Jack Lawson."

"Sheriff," Cal acknowledged. "I've heard plenty about you, but haven't had the pleasure of meeting you before now. All good things. I promise."

Jack smiled and some of the tension went out of his shoulders. Probably no one else noticed but me. "If I believed that, I'm sure you've got some oceanfront property you could sell me too."

Cal nodded, his mouth quirking in amusement. "I figure as an elected official if you're not pissing someone off on a daily basis then you're probably not doing your job. But I've been here a month and see how the county is run from the Sheriff's Department. You do a good job, and the people respect the officers and the department, which is better than you could say for most places.

"From what little I've seen of Bloody Mary, it's a great community, though the name could use some work. And I appreciate the ingenuity of some of the neighbors on my street, trying to see me coming and going. If you're looking for new recruits I'd start there."

"Ha, you're not kidding. Let me know if you want a tour, such as it is. I'll take you around and introduce you. Most people think you're a drug dealer or a kidnapper."

"Only in my undercover days. I'm mostly an upstanding citizen now. Has Detective Lewis had a chance to fill y'all in on what we've got? I have to assume there's a reason Doctor Graves is here at the scene and not working in the ER."

"I'm coroner for the county," I said. "The company is better than it was at the hospital."

"I remember," he said. "I'm glad you got rid of the headache. Everyone grab a hard hat and I'll walk you through."

"I'm going to check in with my men and get reports," Chief Edwards said. "I'm getting too old to wade through the shit. I'll leave that to you young folks." And with that he saluted and walked off.

"You can see why I'm so fond of him," I said.

Jack grinned and elbowed me playfully in the ribs, and I caught the curious expression on Cal's face at our interaction. "You owe me fifty bucks, Graves." He nodded to the silver Honda Civic that had parked in the ditch outside the gates and I sighed in disgust.

Emergency personnel worked quickly to get crime scene tape up so Floyd didn't get too close, but in my mind anything short of being in the next county was too close for me. Floyd was getting closer to forty, but he was probably in the best shape of his life. I always wondered how he managed to find dress shirts to fit around his neck and over his biceps. He wore thick-rimmed glasses and habitually carried a red notebook with him everywhere he went.

"Good morning, Sheriff," Floyd called out. "Care to make a statement?"

"Not at this time, Floyd. I'll make a statement once we have more facts and family has been notified."

"The public has a right to know."

"And they will as soon as we have something to tell them. You wouldn't want to misreport, now would you, Floyd? That wouldn't be responsible journalism."

"Because he's always been so good at that," I mumbled under by breath.

"I could ask different questions," he said, moving as close to the yellow tape as possible. "Like why have a couple of your biggest donors not committed to supporting you for the upcoming election? Is there trouble in paradise? Or maybe they're worried that the poor choices you make in your personal life will affect your job as sheriff."

Floyd's eyes cut to me and he smirked. I'd gotten in the habit over the past few months of carrying a small Beretta with me everywhere I went. After a close call with death at the hands of a madman I'd decided to never be caught without a way to defend myself if need be.

The gun weighed heavy in the holster at the small of my back, and I figured Floyd was damned lucky that I had a pretty straight moral center, otherwise he'd be finding himself with a hole in his foot right about now. I wasn't a moron. Aim to maim. Not to kill.

"To be honest I haven't thought about the election," Jack said. "November is a long way off, and I was elected to do a job. I wouldn't be much of a sheriff if I was out looking for donors in the middle of April instead of serving the people of this county."

"That's a very political answer, Sheriff."

Jack just smiled and we continued on toward the house, leaving Floyd at the perimeter. I don't know how Jack did it—how he always managed to keep his cool despite having to deal with people like Floyd or others who'd rather see those who served fail instead of succeed. Maybe it was partly because he had to be a politician. Jack was elected after all. But I think it said more about the kind of person he was deep down. It's why he'd made a good commander during his S.W.A.T. days and why he made a good boss now for hundreds of employees. He gave them the kind of leadership they could always rely on.

"How does that guy find shirts to fit his neck?" Cal asked. "That's ridiculous."

I snorted out a laugh and the tension was broken. "How many bodies do we have?" I asked.

"Well, that's the problem." We each took a hard hat and put it on. "The Connellis have owned this house for the last seven years—dad, mom, a seventeen year old son, and a thirteen year old daughter."

"So what's the problem?" I asked.

"There are five bodies."

CHAPTER THREE

"That's certainly a problem for someone," I said, eyebrows raised. "Any ideas as to the identity?"

"I was hoping you could tell me," Cal said.

I nodded. "Let's go take a look."

A bricked walkway led to the front of the house and what had been the bottom floor porch. That wasn't the main entrance. The main entrance had been on the second floor, but the exterior stairs that had looked so beautiful from the road no longer existed. I'd seen the house when it was whole, so I knew the porch had wrapped around the entirety of the house on both levels.

I'd never entered a house that had burned before. I wasn't expecting it to still be smoking, with the embers that hadn't been extinguished wafting through the air like demon infested snowflakes.

Parts of the house still shifted, which explained the need for hard hats, and as it shifted, hisses of smoke escaped from the newly exposed areas. Wood and insulation stuck out in all directions, making it a maze to get from one space to the next. I tried to identify the furniture, hoping it would give me some kind of clue as to where I was in the house, but it was hard to tell.

The sight of a porcelain doll gave me pause. The hair and eyelashes were gone, and the face cracked across the cheek and blackened with soot. One blue eye stared blankly, while the other remained closed. A child's possession.

Damp smoke lay like a blanket across my lungs, but the underlying smell of burnt flesh hovered, so you could taste it in the back of your throat. It was a smell that was hard to erase from the memory.

"Watch your step," Cal warned. "The guys came through and tested for the weak areas. You can see where they're marked with the white spray paint. But it never hurts to be careful. There's a partial basement on the left side of the house and part of the upper floor collapsed into it."

It was easier to see where the rooms and second floor had been once we crossed the threshold into the house. The floor was littered with fire eaten furniture, blackened and still dripping wet from the thousands of gallons of water that had been dumped to extinguish the flames. Broken glass from picture frames. An iron bedframe with white paint that had bubbled and peeled in places, the scrollwork ornate enough for a princess—or a cherished daughter.

"We're standing in what was the main entryway," Cal said. "The stairs curved and went up in that direction. There were three bedrooms, all with their own baths, on the upper level. When the second floor collapsed everything seemed to fall pretty evenly, but there's some scatter because of the pressure from the fire hose."

"Were you able to find a starting point?" Jack asked.

"My best guess is the kitchen. It's through here." Cal led us to the right side of the house, where one of the two standing chimneys sat stark and blackened against the bright sun. "I'm going to take some of the equipment back with me to test, but look at that coffeepot."

I realized what he was asking us to see right off. There was a pattern to fire—the way objects reacted to the heat. Some things caught flame and burned to ashes. Others melted, becoming deformed blobs of metal or glass.

The granite countertops had collapsed and broken into large pieces when the cabinets they rested on had burned. Doors hung from hinges haphazardly and the oven looked as if it had barely been touched at all. The refrigerator door had expanded outward, looking bloated and misshapen. But I could at least tell what and where these objects were.

The coffeepot was no more than a blackened mass of fragments. The only way I was able to recognize it at all was because of the metal base that had a small rectangle for the clock. A perfect circle of glass from the bottom of the coffee pot lay on top. There were singe marks on the side of the stainless steel refrigerator, similar to the marks seen after a detonation.

"Deliberate?" I asked.

"I'm not sure at this point. I need to find all the pieces and put it back together. I'll be able to tell then. But it can happen by accident. Sometimes the factory doesn't put protection around the coils and they can get so hot they can combust. And if the Connellis left the coffeepot on by accident or maybe had the automatic timer set, then it could happen. Timing and bad luck often play a big part in fires like this one. Either way, it's going to be a long night for all of us."

"Timing and bad luck and five people dead," I said, shaking my head. "Where are the bodies?"

"Master suite was on the first floor, just off the kitchen. There was very little disturbance back in that area other than the water damage, so the scene is mostly still intact. We'll wrap around to that side last.

"I want you to check out the one on the far side first. It's in a precarious position, and I don't want to take any chances. The floor above the basement is unstable and part of it is missing. When the second floor caved in, one of the bedrooms landed directly on top of that area. We tried to stabilize the body so it didn't fall into the basement, but I can't promise it'll stay that way."

"Thanks for that," I said. "I'd prefer not to spelunk into any smoking holes to retrieve a body."

"We aim to please."

We left the kitchen and went back in the direction we'd come. The house had been massive in size. I hadn't been kidding when I'd compared it to a mini-White House. The curved staircase had broken from the upper floor and fallen to the side before it had burned, but part of the spindles of the railings were still intact. It was fascinating how the fire could reduce one object to ashes but leave another whole.

"The first body is over here," Cal said. "Watch your step and stay on the path we marked. If you breathe wrong something might collapse."

"A comforting thought," I murmured. I took out my camera and turned it on, adjusting the settings for light.

I noticed Martinez was looking a little pale. Most of the cops under Jack hadn't seen too many dead bodies—if any. I knew Martinez wasn't new to death, he'd helped us pin down a killer just a couple weeks back. But there were some who would never be comfortable with death, no matter how many times they saw it.

Jack knew it too. "Lewis, why don't you and Martinez start running backgrounds on the Connellis. I want to know everything about them, including all of their close acquaintances. That fifth body is someone who has a family that needs to be notified."

"Yes, sir," Lewis said, slapping Martinez on the back. "Let's go, junior."

I'd already put Martinez out of my mind. The victim had come into view and it was my only focus now. The right half of the body hung precariously over the ledge into the basement. The skull faced me, the mouth open in a parody of a scream. The fire had ravaged the flesh and muscles, leaving something behind that was almost unrecognizable as human.

I followed the white lines of spray paint, careful to not stray from the path. There wasn't a whole lot of room to work with, so Jack and Cal stood back while I scooted closer to the body, praying I didn't shift any debris and send the body tumbling.

"Victim is male," I said, taking a few pictures. I knelt down and handed my camera back to Jack. A steady stream of water dripped onto my hardhat from somewhere above. "And I'd say somewhere between fifteen to nineteen in age as the epiphyseal plates haven't fully closed."

The movies never depicted burn fatalities correctly. The thing about the human body was that it was pretty dense in places, and really freaking hard to burn in its entirety. The extremities, like fingers and toes—anything that had smaller bones—would burn away. But the torso of a body was thick, so even if the skin was gone, the insides were still viable enough for me to do an autopsy.

"Looks like he was dressed for bed." I was talking more to myself than Cal and Jack at this point. I was in the zone—that faraway place I had to go to when I was studying a body—so it was all about the facts and details and not the person in front of me.

I used a pair of tweezers to pull off what might have been pajama bottoms that had adhered to the skin of the upper thigh. The face was gone, so there was no hope of identifying visually against a photograph, and the fingers were gone as well so no hope of fingerprinting.

"We'll have to identify through dental." I grabbed a small flashlight out of my bag and turned it on. And then I shone the light into the gaping mouth, carefully widening it further so I could see as far down into the throat as possible.

"There's soot and burns in the airway," I said, swabbing the inside of the mouth and nose and putting it in an evidence baggie. "So he was breathing on his own when the fire started."

I labeled the baggie *M1*—Male 1—to

indicate which victim it belonged to and continued to look over the body closely.

"I won't be able to see if there were any perimortem injuries until I can do x-rays. Have the guys go ahead and bag him and get him stabilized. Lets move on to the next one."

"It's right over here," Cal said. "I did a preliminary sketch of the house and the rooms, and then did another sketch of where the rooms fell and into which quadrants of the bottom floor. From my calculations both of these victims were occupying the same room, so when it collapsed they landed in the same general area."

Victim number two was facedown next to what was left of a metal bedframe, and the coils from the inside of the mattress lay blackened between the slats, though the mattress itself was long gone.

"This one is female," I said. "Also fifteen to nineteen years of age."

"Then not the daughter?" Cal asked.

"No, the bones are different in those who are younger. You said she was thirteen. This girl is older. Maybe a girlfriend."

"Oldest kid's girlfriend is sleeping over?" Jack said. "Wow. Lenient parents. My mom would've kicked my ass. And hers too."

"She would've kicked your ass if you'd

gotten caught," I said wryly. "You had plenty of sleepover guests at that age that your mother never knew about."

Jack winked unashamed and I rolled my eyes. I went back to photographing the scene and checking for marks of violence from the back of the skull all the way down. I'd started breathing through my mouth in shallow pants to counteract the smell. It wasn't working, but it was habit anyway.

"I don't miss those days at all," Jack said. "I'm so glad you've helped me mend my wicked ways and gotten me to settle down. Hey, we should get married or something. If you've got time in your schedule, I think Saturday would be good."

"I'm going to help you settle down off a cliff if you don't stop teasing me about the wedding. Help me turn the body."

"You guys are getting married?" Cal asked, bending down next to the stubby legs to help me turn her over. Jack moved across from me to act as a stabilizer. "Congratulations. Finally found someone that could deal with you before coffee, huh, Jaye?"

"There's room for you off that cliff too, Walker."

Jack choked off a laugh and then counted to three. We turned the mystery girl over and

I went through the same process, checking her airway for soot and burns.

"It's the same as the boy," I said. "Soot and burns in the airways. Minus the fibers from her nightclothes. Though it looks like part of the bed sheets are adhered to the skin."

"She was naked?" Jack asked.

"Yeah. You can tell a lot from the fibers. See how the left leg looks like it has a film over it?" I ran a gloved finger over the blackened area of the thigh and used my tweezers to pull back a white plastic-like substance.

"The sheets weren't made of a natural fiber. That's why it's hardened like this. You can see the way the sheet was draped over her and the position she was laying when she died."

"What time was the fire department alerted?" Jack asked Cal.

"Call came through the alarm company at twelve forty-seven. Took them seventeen minutes to respond because we're out in the middle of nowhere. By the time they arrived the whole house was lit up like the Fourth of July."

"Smoke alarms fully functional?"

"Yes, sir," Cal drawled. "They were wired into the alarm system and everything showed as functional from their end."

"I don't know about you, but if my girlfriend is over for the evening and I'm seventeen years old, there's not a chance in hell I'm fast asleep by twelve forty-seven."

"Especially if there's a warm and naked female in the bed next to you," Cal agreed.

"Why?" I asked. "I'm assuming seventeen year old males fall asleep just as quickly as adult males after sex. Why is it out of the realm of possibility they'd both be asleep by that point? Especially on a school night."

Jack and Cal both looked at me like I'd grown a second head.

"You've never been a seventeen year old boy so I'm going to give you the benefit of the doubt. At that age, if you're given the opportunity to have sex and you have a set amount of hours to do it in, then you're not going to waste any of those hours sleeping. It's about opportunity and an unlimited amount of stamina."

Cal nodded in agreement and I figured the two of them would probably know better than anyone.

"So you're saying despite the fact that they have obvious signs of smoke inhalation, which is a normal cause of death in a house fire, you don't think they died of natural causes?"

"I don't know what to think until you come back with the autopsy results," Cal said. "But my gut is telling me something is off, despite the way things are looking from the outside. Preliminary intel we got on Anthony Connelli is that he worked for the Department of Defense. It's worth digging a little deeper just for that reason alone."

"You'll see when you examine the other bodies. Everyone was asleep when the fire started. Everyone is in bed. And no one heard the smoke alarms or the secondary alarms from the house alarm that notified the fire department. The fire started in the kitchen, so maybe the parents are affected by the smoke first and never wake up. But it would take time for the smoke to reach the second floor."

"And say the alarms did wake them and they were trapped on the second floor," Jack broke in. "She's right next to the bed, and we can probably assume the boy was too since he's so close in proximity. Fire victims typically lock themselves in bathrooms or closets or try to jump out the windows to escape the smoke. They don't just lay in bed and let the fire get them."

"So what you're both saying is that you

want me to look really hard for signs of foul play."

"Pretty much," Cal said. "I'd like to be there when you do the autopsies."

"I don't have a problem with that as long as you don't throw up all over my bodies." He looked offended at the suggestion, so I was guessing Cal was okay with getting down and dirty with the messier side of my job. What was yet to be seen was whether or not he could handle the smell of the embalming fluid I used for the mortuary side of my job.

I saw Jack shake his head out of the corner of my eye and knew what he was thinking. Jack could handle just about anything, but a whiff of the embalming fluid was enough to have him going green and running for the nearest exit. I also noticed Jack didn't try to warn Cal. Some things just needed to be learned from experience.

"I'm not going to be able to start the autopsies until tomorrow morning. My freezer only holds four—five in a desperate pinch— and I've got two I need to embalm and move to viewing rooms to make room for the Connellis and guest."

"You lead a fascinating life, Doctor Graves."

"You ain't seen nothing yet, Walker. If I

told you some of the things that have happened over the last year it would turn your hair gray."

"Trouble likes to follow you. You're hell on wheels."

"Yeah, well I traded in my roller skates for a Formula One car. It's getting a lot harder to outrun the flames lately."

I looked down at my watch and winced at the time. I was going to be cutting it close to make the appointment.

"Let's get her bagged and then move to the next body. I have a wedding dress to try on."

CHAPTER FOUR

"Oh, for crying out loud, Jack. I can practically hear you thinking. Why don't you just ask what you want to know instead of waiting for me to volunteer the information?"

"Because it's more entertaining for me to watch you get all worked up about what you think I might be thinking." He squeezed my thigh playfully and I narrowed my eyes at him.

We were headed back to Bloody Mary so Vaughn and I could drive to Richmond to the bridal shop. It was about ten minutes until three o'clock. Which meant I was going to be very late and Vaughn was probably going to fill my trousseau with nothing by granny gowns and yellow clothing. Yellow made me look like a corpse, so this was a genuine concern.

The EMS vans had left with the bodies about twenty minutes before us, and hopefully everyone was getting unloaded and situated in my lab. I had a very short window of time to work with before the bodies started decomposing, so I needed to deal with the wedding dress and then go embalm Chloe Sanders and Bernie Harrison. Though I was thinking I should probably refrain from telling the ladies at the bridal shop that when explaining why I needed them to hurry.

I slipped my sunglasses off the top of my head and onto my nose. "You're right. I don't know why I'm getting so worked up about it. If you're not curious, then I won't press the issue. We missed lunch."

I checked the clock on the dashboard and wondered since I was going to be late anyway if we could swing through the drive-thru.

I saw Jack's lips twitch at my response, and I knew I hadn't fooled him with my nonchalance. "I could eat," he finally said. "As long as it's not barbecue. I'm thinking of becoming a vegetarian after today."

I pretty much felt the same way, so I couldn't argue. Even bacon didn't sound all that appealing.

"You told me about Walker, you know."

I pressed my lips together to keep from denying it right off the bat, and then I tried to think back and remember. I didn't remember much about my time with Cal, other than the fact I worked like a fiend and the sex was great. It was outside the bedroom we had issues. And I honestly didn't know how much of that relationship I'd shared with Jack. Mostly because I was always embarrassed that I could never be in a relationship with a man that wanted to stick.

More than one man had said that I was intimidating. That I didn't let them be the man in the relationship. Which I found confusing because I didn't know how to be any other way. I was independent and always approached a relationship as if we were equals.

There was a weird dividing line in my mind. Ever since Jack and I had become lovers instead of just friends everyone before him just kind of faded into the background. We'd been best friends for so many years—we knew just about everything about each other, with the exception of things we'd each done in our respective jobs that we weren't ready to share, and might not ever be ready to share.

"Is this one of those times where you're

trying to do reverse psychology and I end up telling you everything you want to know anyway? Because I don't remember having that conversation with you."

"You never told me his name, but I recognized him from the way you described him. Do you remember what you said?"

"Apparently not. Clearly I have amnesia about every man I ever dated before you."

"Then my work here is done," he grinned. "No, but seriously. He moved in with you for a little while. And the day he moved in you called me and said, "Jack, I don't know why I'm doing this. He's not for me. At least not as more than a friend.""

I remembered now and turned my head to look out the window at the passing landscape.

"You remember what you said next?"

"I don't know why you're asking me. Your brain is like a damned computer."

"I'll take that to mean you want me to continue." He'd taken my hand and was rubbing it in slow, soothing circles. "You said, "He's not for me. But I'm not sure anyone is, so maybe I should just make do for as long as it lasts. It's the loneliness that's the worst. I can live with knowing I haven't found my soulmate if it means I don't have to be alone.""

I bit my bottom lip and it all came rushing

back. That feeling of loneliness that had plagued me during those years I'd been away from home and Jack, working my ass off through medical school and then at the hospital. I'd lost my sense of self during that time.

"And in my head I was thinking, you silly girl. I'm right here. I've always been right here. But you had to discover that for yourself. And I knew that."

He squeezed my hand and I choked out a laugh that sounded more like a sob. "Yeah, well I've been known to be a dumbass on occasion. Just ask Vaughn." I made sure I blinked the tears back and then found the courage to look at him. "Thanks for waiting for me, Jack. You were worth it."

"We've got a lifetime, babe. Everything before was just leading up to this moment. Including the Cal Walkers and Lauren Rhodes in our pasts." Lauren had been an ex-girlfriend of Jack's. She worked for the Department of Justice and our paths had crossed during a case. "But if he tries to make a move on you, I'll have to kill him. Just so you know."

"I'll make sure he gets the memo to keep his distance."

Jack turned onto Catherine of Aragon and

headed all the way to the opposite end where the funeral home was located. There wasn't much happening at that end of the block. There'd been a strip mall across the street, but all the businesses had gone under except for the Laundromat.

The recession had hit Bloody Mary hard. The businesses that had survived had picked up shop and moved into the Towne Square to reach more customers. The ones that hadn't survived had sold everything they could and closed their doors. The strip mall across the street was just a sad reminder, though I'd heard rumor that a new church was going to rent out the space for Sunday services.

Graves Funeral Home was a three story brick Colonial that had been built by my great-grandparents more than sixty years ago. The walls of that house had seen a lot of death, including that of my great-grandmother, who'd jumped out the third story window. Though there were many, including the sheriff at the time, who thought she'd been pushed by my great-grandfather. I'd known my great-grandfather, so I wouldn't have put it past him. He was a real peach.

The Graves name left a hell of a legacy. The men were con-artists, thieves, and assholes. The women tended to die early.

Either by their plan or God's. I was hoping to break the tradition, but I was running low on my nine lives. Like I'd told Cal, I'd had a hell of a year.

The front of the funeral home was flanked by two massive oak trees—the roots gnarled and crawling out of the ground like bony fingers and the branches heavy with leaves and arching low. A bricked sidewalk ran from the street to the massive front doors, but only those visiting their loved ones used the front entry. Most people came in and out through the side door under the carport.

The EMS vans were backed in under the portico and a Tahoe from the Sheriff's Department blocked them in. Vaughn's Mercedes was parked on the street and Jack pulled in behind it.

A house fire that killed an entire family would be big news, and it was obvious word had already spread because well-meaning citizens were standing along the sidewalks, talking on their phones and relaying what was happening to their best friends or relatives as the bodies were unloaded and taken inside.

"I haven't seen this kind of crowd since the Christmas parade," I said.

"You know how much Bloody Mary likes to share in a sense of community. At least no one is selling hot dogs."

"Actually, I wouldn't mind that so much. I'm starving. You got mushy in the car and forgot to drive through somewhere."

Jack grasped both sides of my flannel shirt and pulled me across the seat, his lips crashing down on mine. There was tongue involved and a moan or two. And by the time Jack pulled away I'd forgotten all about being hungry and remembered how excited I was for our upcoming honeymoon.

My heart was pounding and my breathing heavy, and I sat in the seat dazed for a minute, trying to remember how to do the simple tasks in life, like unbuckling my seatbelt and opening the car door.

"Sorry about the mushiness. Is my man card still intact?"

"Oh, yeah," I sighed. "Feel free to be as mushy as you'd like. I'll tolerate it because I love you. That's what sacrifice is."

We grinned at each other like fools and I opened the car door, sliding to the ground. I grabbed my bag and slung it over my shoulder.

"It's going to be a late night for both of us," Jack said. "Call me when you're done here and I'll swing by and pick you up. Hopefully we'll have a better idea of the identity of our fifth victim by end of day."

"10-4, buttercup. Keep me posted."

My hand was on the door ready to push it closed when two more vehicles parked behind Jack. One was a silver Lexus SUV. The other was a white panel van. The Lexus belonged to Jack's mother. I had no idea who was in the panel van, but when three women got out and started hauling large garment bags and sewing cases, I had a pretty good idea.

"We knew you'd be late, dear," Jack's mother called out. "There's no point in having all this money if you can't make things more convenient, so we're coming to you. Now get inside and strip down so you can deal with your dead."

I saw one of the dress shop girls sway and she paled as she eyed all the activity going in and out of the funeral home. I smiled and winked at Jack. "This might be fun after all."

"Bad girl, Doctor Graves," he said, shaking his head with a smile.

I waved him off and then followed Mrs. Lawson's instructions. She'd walloped my behind on more than one occasion as a child, and I wouldn't put it past her to do it now that I was an adult.

CHAPTER FIVE

Mrs. Lawson was a force to be reckoned with, and she'd been more of a parent to me than my mother had. I knew what parental love was supposed to feel like because of her, and I loved her as if she were my own.

I had such weird feelings about my parents. They were my parents, so there was that familial loyalty that was almost ingrained. And there were plenty of good memories to go along with the bad. I'd never been mistreated, but their love for each other had always been greater than their love for me. And their preoccupation with the illegal extracurricular activities they'd been involved in had left me with a lot of alone time in the house by myself, sometimes for days. And sometimes I wouldn't see them for weeks, so Jack would come get me and I'd pack a bag to stay at the Lawson house.

It was through Jack's parents I'd gotten to see what a real family should be like. Mr. and Mrs. Lawson loved each other and they loved the child they'd made together. They had fun and did things on weekends. And they disciplined with a firm hand if needed, but always with love. Sometimes I'd stand back and just watch them as a unit, separating myself from the equation, and wonder at that palpable love. How they'd just grin at each other for no reason and know that they'd always be there for each other, through the good times and bad.

Mrs. Lawson was a small woman, maybe an inch over five feet, with small, elegant bones and a petite frame. She was in her mid-fifties but looked much younger. Her hair was as dark as Jack's, but where his eyes were dark like his father's, Mrs. Lawson's were a pale, clear blue. Her size had never kept her from accomplishing anything she wanted to. Including getting me to strip down to nothing and stand on the dais in viewing room three.

"I've got to say, this is awkward." I resisted the urge to cover my bare breasts with my arm while one of the women—her name was Marguerite—wrapped a measuring tape around my waist and hips. "I usually don't get naked in front of people until I've known them for at least twenty minutes."

"I used to be that way too, darling," Mrs. Lawson said. "You'll get less picky as you get older. Especially if you're going through menopause. One day you'll find yourself naked in the frozen food aisle of the Piggly Wiggly and have no recollection of how you got there." She winked and went back to examining the veils that another one of the women had whipped out of her bag.

"I'm certainly looking forward to that," I said. "Because I haven't given people enough to talk about in this town."

"They'd talk no matter what you did. Might as well make it interesting." She pursed her lips in concentration. "I just don't know about these veils."

I wasn't too sure either. I wasn't much of a veil person. Or a wedding dress person for that matter. But I figured I'd let the more experienced folks make the decisions.

"Your body is quite nice for someone your age," Marguerite told me. She was a small Hispanic woman somewhere between the age of forty-five and ninety. "Of course that'll all change the moment you have children."

"That's the God's honest truth," Mrs. Lawson said. "But they're mostly worth it. Except for the times they're not. And then the best medicine is a healthy glass of wine and a hot bath. Remember these talks, Jaye. You're like a daughter to me, so I want you to be prepared."

"You're certainly making me want to start a family right away. I don't know what's been holding us back." I said it straight-faced and Mrs. Lawson chuckled. "Are we almost done here?"

Marguerite rolled her eyes. "You haven't even tried the dress on yet. And you've lost weight since the initial fitting."

"It's been a busy week. Everyone waited to die until right before my wedding."

"You're a strange girl. What kind of woman spends all her time with dead people?"

"One that doesn't particularly like to talk to living people. Except for Jack. Which is why I'm marrying him."

I wasn't a delicate kind of girl. I knew how to work hard and get my hands dirty. I'd grown up with four guys for best friends and learned to do all the stuff guys like to do. I could swear with the best of them and out sarcasm any of the cops. It's not that there weren't times when I enjoyed being or looking more feminine—dressing up for dinner or surprising Jack with pretty lingerie—it's just that my career and Bloody Mary didn't give me the opportunity that often.

So when the two other ladies came at me with a contraption of horror and squeezed me into it—touching me in places I was pretty sure my gynecologist hadn't—I wondered how close to the door I could get before Mrs. Lawson tackled me to the ground.

"Don't even think about it, Jaye."

I sighed—or would have if I could've taken a breath. I turned and looked at myself in the mirror they'd propped against the wall and my mouth dropped open.

"Holy crap. Look at my boobs." I reached up to feel them to make sure they were really mine. "I could hurt someone with these puppies." My hands trailed down the lacy contraption, marveling at the smallness of my waist and the flare of my hips. "This is pure deception. The lingerie industry should be ashamed of themselves."

"All the way to the bank, I'm sure," Mrs. Lawson said. "And it's not deception. It's just amplifying the assets you already have. It's like when you drink coffee in the morning. Your brain is already in your head. But the coffee makes sure you can use it to the best of your ability."

"I guess when you put it like that—not to mention it'll knock Jack's socks off."

"And the rest of his clothes if you're doing it right."

"Good grief," I said, watching my cheeks flush red in the mirror. "I can't talk about this with you. He's your son."

"Girl, you were talking about this stuff with me when you were sixteen and stupid with it. And again at twenty-one, twenty-four, and thirty if my memory serves me right. At least now you're doing it with the right man. And word on the street is he's pretty good at it, so thank your lucky stars. I know plenty of women who've been stuck with a man who wouldn't know a clitoris if it was attached to their forehead. There's a reason half the kids in this town look like Billy McQueen."

I pinched my lips tight and glanced at the door again in hopes of escape. Those bodies were starting to look more appealing by the second.

Almost as if I'd conjured it, Vaughn knocked and stuck his head in.

"Damn, woman. You could put someone's eye out with those things." His brows rose almost to his hairline as he came all the way inside and shut the door behind him. "How have I known you for more than thirty years and never realized you had breasts before?"

"To be fair, have you ever noticed that any woman has breasts?"

"An excellent point. Yours are lovely, by the way. I brought you a sandwich and a cup of coffee. Jack said you hadn't eaten."

"God, I love that man."

"Umm…I made you the sandwich. How about a little credit where credit is due."

"I love you too. Now please give me that sandwich before I hurt you."

"Not until after you try the dress on," Mrs. Lawson said. "That's all you need is a mustard stain down the front of your wedding gown."

"It'll be very avant-garde," Vaughn said. "A new trend in designer wedding gowns everywhere."

"It'll look like Jaye spilled mustard on her wedding gown," she said, exasperated. "I swear every hair on my head I have to color is because of you kids."

"Can we just put the gown on?" I asked. "I can smell that coffee and I'm not above killing everyone in this room for it and shoving you all in my freezer."

Marguerite and the other ladies gasped, their eyes wide and mouths hanging open.

"She can be a real bitch without coffee," Vaughn said. "But she won't kill anyone. She doesn't have any more room in the freezer, so you're safe."

I snickered and waited while Marguerite unzipped the garment bag and pulled out the dress. It was a long column of delicate lace and silk, and I immediately broke out in a sweat. I couldn't remember the last time I made it through a day without getting blood or something else on my clothes. I couldn't imagine what I'd do to that beautiful white dress.

I guess it wasn't really white—more of a creamy color that Marguerite said would complement my skin better than stark white. I'd been adamant about not wearing anything poofy or that made me resemble a whipped dessert. I was a doctor, for Christ's sake. I wanted to get married with a little dignity.

One of the ladies held out a hand so I could keep my balance and I stepped carefully into the dress. I held my breath as she pulled it up, wondering when I'd become the kind of person to let someone else dress me. I slipped my arms into the lacy cap sleeves and then waited for the final result as she fastened the long row of buttons down my back. It suddenly became very obvious why I needed someone to dress me.

"Oh, Jaye. How lovely." Mrs. Lawson's eyes were damp and her hands were clasped in front of her chest.

I was afraid to look. That fear and the butterflies rumbling in my stomach were exactly what had me raising my chin and meeting my gaze in the mirror. I almost didn't recognize myself.

Mrs. Lawson had been right about the lingerie. It just emphasized what was already there, so the sleek column of lace hugged curves I didn't know I had. The dress had a nostalgic feel to it—something that would have been worn during my great-grandmother's era—but it seemed to fit me. A healthy bit of cleavage showed in the front and a small train pooled behind me.

"I don't think you need the veil," Mrs. Lawson said. "Simple is best. Do you have your mother's pearls?"

"They're in the safe deposit box," I answered. "But I'm not wearing them." I wasn't one to place a lot of importance on symbols or superstition, but I didn't want anything to taint my day with Jack. And that included memories of my parents.

Mrs. Lawson nodded and said, "You'll wear mine then. The dress calls for them." She clapped her hands together and the spell seemed to break, putting everyone in motion again.

Marguerite pinned a couple of places that needed to be hemmed, and then the dress was whisked away and I was left in nothing but the corset.

"This is my cue to leave," Vaughn said. "I promised you food and I delivered. And I also promised you wouldn't have to do anything else for the wedding. Which is mostly true, but I might have fibbed a little about that. I hope to God you like pink taffeta. We found a sale over at Big Lots and wiped them out of everything."

My eyes widened and I stood there in shock. I'd never been a fan of pink. But then I realized Vaughn was joking when Mrs. Lawson slapped him in the stomach.

"Don't listen to him, Jaye. There won't be anything pink in sight. Now eat and go see to your dead. I don't mean to speak ill of the deceased, but the entire downstairs smells like a barbecue. It's a little off putting."

One of Marguerite's helpers ran toward the bathroom, gagging, and I took a bite of sandwich, trying to remember a time when death had wreaked havoc with my senses that way. The answer was never. When death was a part of your life from childhood you became conditioned to it. And I knew that conditioning made me great at my job. I wasn't sure about how great of a person it made me though.

CHAPTER SIX

It was well past eight o'clock by the time I finished embalming Chloe Sanders and Bernie Harrison.

I had a couple of interns from the college that helped me out from time to time, and I'd decided to leave the prep work for the interment to them to deal with the next day. I cleaned up the mess and disposed of all the waste, and then I covered both bodies with sheets and left them on the stainless steel tables I used for embalming.

I was long past the point of exhausted. The last twelve hours had been non-stop, both physically and emotionally. But I had room in my freezer to move the Connelli family inside. And if I played an interesting game of Tetris with the stretchers I could fit in the mystery girl too.

I normally showered and changed clothes after I embalmed bodies because of the smell, but I texted Jack that I was finished and was pleasantly surprised to see him text back immediately that he was waiting in the driveway.

I washed my hands and did one last glance through the lab to make sure I hadn't forgotten anything, then made my way up the narrow metal stairs to the first floor.

"Hey," I said, surprised to see Jack waiting for me in the kitchen.

"Hey, yourself."

He looked me over from head to toe, and I knew he was assessing whether or not I'd overdone it. I'd had a couple of close calls with death over the past several months, and when added to the stress of what I'd gone through after my parents' deaths and the following FBI investigation, it was safe to say I'd let my physical and mental health suffer.

I had a tendency to let myself work past the point of exhaustion, and when I did it was a little harder to keep those demons that plagued me at bay. It was easy to get mired in the muck of my own thoughts, wanting nothing more than to hide under the covers and never come out.

But Jack was my light. Just as I knew I was his. He had his own demons to deal with.

"Long day," he said, opening his arms for a hug.

"I smell like embalming fluid. You probably want to keep your distance."

He grabbed my hand and pulled me into the embrace. "I'll try not to throw up in your hair. Now come here and be still for a minute."

He wrapped his arms around me and I felt his warmth seep through to my bones. I hadn't realized I was cold. I put my arms around his waist and rested my head on his chest and just let him hold me. No demands. No talk of work or weddings. Just comfort.

My eyes felt heavy and I realized if I didn't get moving again that I was likely to fall asleep standing up. I loved that I was able to drop my guard with Jack. That I didn't always have to be so tough. So strong.

"I love you," I said, raising my head so I could look him in the eyes. "I don't think I've told you that today."

He smiled and kissed the tip of my nose. "I never get tired of hearing it. Now lets go home and get showered. I'm not sure how much longer I can keep the promise to not throw up. And if you don't mind, we'll ride home with the windows down."

I rolled my eyes, but I was smiling again and felt a little lighter of heart. By the time we got home I was thinking more about putting food in my stomach than I was thinking about sleep, so I knew I had another few hours left in me to help Jack. He wouldn't stop working until we'd done everything we could to find out if the Connellis had been murdered or just victims of an unfortunate accident.

"You find out anything about our fifth victim?" I asked once we were inside.

We dumped our bags on the foyer table and Jack dropped his keys in the bowl, and then we headed upstairs.

"When I got back to the office a missing persons report had been filed on a Cassandra Owens. Her parents called her Cassie. According to them she was working on a group project for school with Damian Connelli—that's the oldest boy—and another kid named Michael Bruce. Lewis and Martinez talked to them because I was stuck in a meeting with my internal affairs guy on an ongoing case, so I didn't get to speak with them."

Sometimes it was easy to forget that Jack was responsible for the entire Sheriff's

Department and that he had to see to everything from the top to the bottom. He was always connected to his men and he delegated as much as possible, but there were some things only Jack could do.

"They knew she was spending the night?"

"Yeah, apparently it wasn't an uncommon occurrence."

"So where was Michael Bruce?"

"That's the question. There was no one at home when we sent officers by, and we've hit a block with cell phone numbers because his father is a Senator. It's possible we overlooked Bruce's body when we went through this morning. Walker is going to rig up a pulley system and send a man down into the basement to look for him."

"Busy day."

"And tomorrow is going to get busier. The Owens gave us dental records, so you can do a comparison for identification."

I stripped to the skin and put my clothes in one of the plastic bags I kept beneath the sink in the master bathroom. If I didn't contain them the entire room would be permeated with the smell of embalming fluid.

The master bathroom room was probably my favorite room in the house. The kitchen was pretty amazing too, but I was mostly useless there unless Jack needed me to boil water or alphabetize the contents of the pantry.

The bathroom was the size of my old bedroom—the one I'd slept in before I'd moved in with Jack—and one entire wall was a special glass that looked out over the trees and down to the water below. I'd spent a lot of time in the Jacuzzi tub with a book, and if time wasn't of the essence I'd have sunk to my shoulders and let the day melt away.

I turned on the shower and leaned my head against the cold tile while I waited for it to warm up, and I noticed Jack getting undressed out of the corner of my eye.

"You looked like you needed help scrubbing your back," he said, grinning unrepentantly.

I recognized the look in his eyes and my blood hummed beneath my skin. It was amazing how awake and revived I could get after just one look. "Better be careful. The majority of household accidents occur in the bathroom."

"Darling, I'm a cop. Careful is my middle name."

"That's funny," I said, wide-eyed. "I thought it was Oliver."

His smile promised retribution, and he

shed the rest of his clothes efficiently and with purpose.

"It looks like you got your second wind." I arched a brow at his obvious arousal, and then took a step back when he stalked toward me, my ass bumping into the wall. There was no part of Jack's body that was soft, from the thick muscles in his thighs up to those little indents above his hips that drove me crazy, and up further still to the strong shoulders and arms that could hold me so gently.

"That smart mouth of yours drives me crazy." He placed both hands on either side of my face and then leaned in, teasing me with nipping kisses along my bottom lip.

"That's probably a good thing, since you'll be hearing from it the next fifty years or so."

Plumes of mist from the hot water billowed out the open shower door and fogged the mirrors and glass. Jack kept up the teasing, making my head spin, and moved my body until the spray of hot water hit my shoulders.

His hands slid down my slicked back and followed the curve of my ass, lifting me against him, and I moaned as his mouth took mine completely. Jack was a thorough lover and took his time. It was always me that was impatient.

He took the time to wash my hair,

supporting my head to keep the soap out of my eyes. And then he lathered body wash in his hands and smoothed them over my heated skin, starting at my shoulders and massaging his way down my back.

I was in that half-dream/half-reality state that only intimacy could bring. Where my legs couldn't quite support me and my head was spinning. My senses were heightened—the sound of the water as it pounded over us—the smell of soap—the taste of Jack's mouth on mine—the feel of his calloused fingers driving me past the point of control.

"Please, Jack," I begged. "I need you." It was all I had to say.

His mouth devoured, his tongue stroking mine, and he walked me toward the back of the shower until I hit the wall. My leg hitched around his hip and I stood on the ball of my other foot as I felt him probe against me.

Again, he teased me. The fullness of him pressing against my opening only to retreat again. The cry that broke in my throat was a sob of frustration, and he laughed into my mouth, though it was strained.

"God, Jaye." He gripped my wrists with one hand and turned me around, so my face was against the tile, and then he slid inside me with one long stroke and I forgot how to breathe.

Jack let go of my wrists and his hands stroked down the smooth length of my back until they reached my hips. And then his fingers found purchase and he rode me hard, until I was screaming for release and mercy with the same breath.

His hand curved around my hip until he touched the very core of me, and that was all it took to send me flying over the edge of surrender. He kissed the base of my neck and followed.

CHAPTER SEVEN

"Am I dead?" I asked.

"Only if you keep laying with your head under the shower spray like that. How are you even breathing?"

We'd somehow ended up sprawled on the floor of the shower. I could hear the laughter in Jack's voice and he pushed me from beneath the spray. I sucked in a deep breath and attempted to open my eyes. Everything was out of focus and I couldn't feel my legs.

"You're good for a man's ego, my love."

All I could manage was a thumbs up sign, and then my hand dropped onto my stomach.

Jack slapped my thigh and said, "Come on, woman. This floor is getting cold and I'm hungry."

I could practically feel the energy zinging off Jack. Orgasms had a tendency to have that effect on him. I, on the other hand, was content to stay where I was and face the possibility of accidental drowning.

"Do I have to fix you dinner as payment for sex?" I asked.

"God, I hope not. I want to live."

Jack managed to get to his feet and then leaned down and hauled me up under my arms. I wobbled in his arms and waited to see if my legs were going to start working or if I was going to walk like John Wayne for the foreseeable future.

"Hey, I can make a sandwich," I said. "I was trying to be wifely."

"We all have our strengths, love. Yours are in every other place except for the kitchen."

He guided me out of the shower and dried me off, wrapping a towel around me before doing the same to himself.

"You're very handy to have around. Let's get married so I can keep you forever and ever."

He smacked me on the butt and guided me into the bedroom. "You'll not get me off task." He tossed a pair of underwear, a pair of jeans, and a long sleeve white Henley tee into my lap. "Clothes. Food. Hungry."

"That's very caveman of you. Sexy." I dressed quickly and towel dried my hair, running my fingers through it to smooth it in place, and then we headed downstairs to the kitchen.

"Do you have the file on Cassandra Owens?" I asked, while he was assembling sandwiches.

"The top file in my bag. Just bring the whole thing."

I retrieved the bag and pulled out the file labeled with Cassandra's name. Her school picture was at the top of the stack and I looked into the eyes of a girl who'd never reach full adulthood. Just by looking at the shape of her face and the bone structure, I had a gut feeling that Cassandra Owens was the mystery girl currently occupying my freezer.

I ran my finger along the features of her picture—dark blond hair and a softness to her cheeks that only the young had. Her eyes were cornflower blue and she'd lined them with dark eyeliner, making her look older than she was. Her eyes held both innocence and womanly knowledge. Her smile was bright, confident—a smile waiting to take on the whole world.

"Seventeen years old," I said. "Third in her

class at Downton Academy—a prep school for the rich and almost famous. Lots of politicians' kids. Tuition prices per year cost as much as all of med school."

Jack put a sandwich in front of me and I took a bite absently. The cobwebs from our earlier bout of sex had cleared and my mind was back to sharp focus. I skimmed through the other pages in the file—mostly academic—and then glanced at her medical files.

"She suffered a broken femur," I said, holding up a copy of the x-ray. "I'll look for that as a backup identifier once we look at dental." I closed the file and looked up at Jack.

He sighed and finished off his sandwich. "You're going to start on her tonight, aren't you?"

"Might as well. The Owens deserve to know if that's their daughter as soon as possible. It'll only take a couple of hours. I'll be back before midnight." I shrugged and looked at him apologetically. "Probably."

"I'll go with you. I want to see if you find anything."

"You think we should invite Cal? He asked to observe."

"He can observe tomorrow. It'd be

awkward for him to see all that beard burn on your neck."

I slapped a hand to my neck and then went to look at my reflection in a small grouping of mirrors hanging just inside the kitchen door.

"Every time. You're like a damned animal marking your territory."

Jack's smile was predatory. "We can play king of the mountain later. Let's go give Cassandra Owens her identity."

I'd never been bothered by being surrounded by the dead in the middle of the night. It's not like it being day or night outside had any effect—dead was dead—though I guess there was a certain macabre feel to the place in the darkness. More so than usual. Maybe it was because there was a quietness to the dark that the daylight didn't have—a hushed stillness.

We didn't have to worry about gawkers at this time of night. All of the businesses except for the café were shut down by eight o'clock every evening, so most people were tucked safely into their homes unless there was a school sporting event. Summers tended to get a little wilder—sometimes people stayed out until after ten—but those were the hell raisers and Jezebels.

Jack parked under the portico and I was already out of the car by the time he turned off the ignition. I was itching to get started. The thought of what Mr. and Mrs. Owens must be going through—the not knowing—is what drove me. It was always the living that suffered, and if I could ease that suffering I would.

I punched in the key code for the basement and the fortified metal door opened with a soft snick. The smell of the embalming fluid I'd used earlier wafted toward us. Jack's face went pale and he swallowed a couple of times. I'd grown up with the smell, so it had never affected me like it did others.

"You okay?" I asked.

"I'm fine. Just give me a second. It'll pass." It was always reassuring to know that Jack, who seemed to be invincible on a day to day basis, was human after all. It was a weakness only I knew about, and I'd take the secret to the grave.

I flicked on the lights and then hit the button for the exhaust fan. The fluorescent lights came on one by one and the smell slowly dissipated as it was sucked up into the fans. Jack and I headed down, our footsteps echoing on the industrial metal stairs and disturbing the quiet.

I went to the freezer and punched in a second code. I'd left mystery girl in the front because I knew I'd more than likely be examining her first, so I rolled her out and over to my workspace. I put on a dark blue smock and tied the string twice around my waist, and then I put a plastic apron on top of that and my white lab coat on top of that.

"You want help lifting her?" Jack asked, grabbing one end of the sterile white sheet so we could transfer her to the work table I used for autopsies.

"On three," I said. I could have moved her myself. The bulk of the weight of her was gone. But it was still easier with Jack's help because the sheets tended to get bunched when I tried to move someone on my own.

We got her transferred over and I flipped on the bright lights over the table, and then I attached my recorder to the lapel of my lab coat. Jack took the stool from under the counter and made himself comfortable. He knew to stay silent and out of the way.

I turned on the recorder and began cataloging the victim. "Female," I said. "Burns on one hundred percent of the body. Left leg ends at the end of the femur. Right leg ends just below patella, though patella is missing.

Right arm ends at humeral lateral epicondyle. Left arm ends at humeral lesser tubercle."

I wrapped her in the sheet she was laying on and then used the pulley system I'd had installed above the table to lift her and record her weight. And then I measured from the top of the skull to what was left of her legs to record the height.

"Height while living is estimated to be just over five feet five inches tall."

I put on a pair of magnifying glasses and brought the light down lower so I could look over the body more carefully. The skin had been ravaged, so looking for birthmarks or other telling signs was almost pointless, but sometimes you got lucky so I did it anyway. I found what I was looking for when I reached the fatty part of the right buttock.

"Anything in her file about a tattoo?" I asked Jack. The top layers of skin had been burned away, but tattoo needles and ink went deep, and I could see the dark staining through my lens.

"Nothing that I read, but it'll be easy enough to find out. She'd have to have parental consent since she's not eighteen."

I hmmmed and moved on, documenting the mark and its location. I removed fibers and more of the melted bed sheet from the back of her body and bagged them.

"Let's go ahead and get x-rays and then we'll get to the good stuff."

"Only you would classify using a stryker saw as the good stuff."

I handed Jack a lead vest and set up the x-ray, starting with dental first and then moving to the rest of the body.

"Hand me those original x-rays from her file would you?" I put up the dental x-rays on the light board and then took the one Jack handed me and placed it next to it. "We've got a match." But just to be sure I compared the x-rays of the femur break she'd had from childhood.

"Victim is identified as Cassandra Owens," I said into the recorder. "Both dental and medical x-rays confirm."

"I'll meet with the parents first thing in the morning," Jack said.

I glanced at the clock and winced. I wasn't going to make the midnight deadline of getting home like I'd promised Jack. Now that we had an identity, the rest of the autopsy was routine. I took blood and vaginal samples and then took another swab of the nose and throat.

"Indication of sexual activity," I said. "I'll take a sample from Damian Connelli and send it off to make sure it's a match."

And then I went about the task of opening Cassandra Owens up to see what was inside.

"How's she look?" Jack asked.

"Healthy. Everything is registering as normal. I don't see any signs of foul play here, Jack. Smoke inhalation seems to be cause of death. It could just be a terrible accident. I'm going to need dental and medical records for the Connelli family too."

"You'll get them. I'm turning into a pumpkin, Doc. Lets put Ms. Owens back together and go home."

"That's the second best offer I've had today."

CHAPTER EIGHT

The next morning came entirely too soon in my opinion.

It was rare that I woke before Jack, but he still slept softly beside me, his body relaxed and his face unguarded. Even in sleep he touched me, his arm draped across my hip and his leg wedged between my thighs.

We were getting married in two days and I had seven dead bodies inside my funeral home. The math wasn't all that favorable as far as saying "I do" and then getting the heck out of Dodge for a week of sex and relaxation. I couldn't leave Bloody Mary without clearing the slate for work.

The viewings for my two embalmed guests were later in the evening, and their funeral services were scheduled at different times the following day. Which meant in between autopsies I needed to remember to make sure the viewing rooms were set up, flowers were ordered, the bodies were well presented, and I was dressed professionally without bodily fluids staining my clothes.

"I can feel you staring at me," Jack said, keeping his eyes closed.

"I figured if I did it long enough you'd wake up and put the coffee on. And maybe bring me a cup in bed."

His eyes cracked open at that request. "I thought that was the wife's job."

"I won't be a wife for three more days, so I figured I should take advantage while I can."

"I also just remembered how bad your coffee is, so maybe cross that off your list of wifely duties."

"I didn't realize there was a list."

"I'll send you a copy. I've got them all written down."

"That's very—organized of you. And potentially dangerous."

Jack grinned. "I like to live on the edge."

"What's on this list of so called duties?" I asked.

"You know. The usual stuff." His hand tightened on my hip and he rolled me to my back, settling between my legs. He rubbed his beard across my neck and then kissed it to soothe. "Laundry. House cleaning. Greeting me at the door in nothing but your lab coat and those high heels you wore for New Year's Eve a couple of years ago."

"I didn't realize you had role playing fantasies."

"I have J.J. Graves fantasies. I don't care what you're wearing as long as it's me."

My breath caught as he slid deep inside of me. That was my favorite part of sex—that first joining—the becoming one flesh. I also loved watching Jack, the way his eyes dilated and the brown bled to black. And how his lids half-closed and the veins in his neck stood out as he braced himself above me.

The loving was long and slow and sweet, with soft caresses and deep kisses. This was what being truly connected felt like. My heart pumped faster, the blood rushed in my ears, and sweat dampened my skin. Jack's hands intertwined with mine and my back arched as the tingles of release raced down my spine and across my skin.

"Jack," I cried out as wave after wave crashed through me. He buried his head against my neck and followed.

It was still shy of seven o'clock by the time we showered. I came out of the bathroom dressed in a towel and went to the big walk in closet Jack and I shared. I pulled out plain white cotton underwear and a matching bra and then stood in front of the rack of clothes. I needed to be comfortable and professional. It was going to be a long day.

I picked black ankle pants and a sweater set in deep purple. The layering was important because the funeral home was always set to colder temperatures. I slipped on black ballet flats for the day and grabbed a pair of black heels for the evening viewings to shove in my bag.

I didn't bother with makeup, but I had supplies at the funeral home and I'd spruce up a little before family members and friends of the deceased started showing up.

My phone buzzed from the nightstand where it was plugged in and I went over to check it as Jack came out of the bathroom, freshly shaved and a towel draped low on his hips.

"It's Walker," I said, reading the text. "He's back at the scene and says he won't be free until noon, so to go ahead without him and he'll catch up when he can."

"That works out. You can come with me to notify the Owens."

I stared at Jack, but he wasn't making eye contact. He normally wore jeans and button down shirts to work, but he pulled out charcoal slacks and a Sheriff's Department polo with the insignia over the left breast.

"You know I hate doing the notifications," I said. "Seriously, I've got too much work to do."

"I hate doing them too, but you know it helps to hear exactly how you identified the victim. They always question the results, and you being there alleviates that."

I put my hands on my hips and made a face. "Dammit."

I knew he was right, but that didn't mean I liked it. Watching the stages of people's grief, as they finally understood that their child was never coming back, was an awful thing to see. And it tore at me every time I had to make one of these visits. It was all fine and good to tell myself to keep distant and not think of the victims as human beings, but that was shot all to hell when faced with the living.

Jack squeezed my shoulder as he passed by to get his gun belt from the top of the closet. He strapped it on and then clipped his badge to the belt.

"Let's ride, Doc. The sooner we get there the sooner we can be done."

"If you drive-thru and buy me a cup of coffee we'll call it even on strong-arming me to come with you to do the notification. And probably I won't want to stab you in the face on the drive."

"Hey, I'm an accommodating man."

Lance and Helen Owens lived in Alexandria, which was a good hour fifteen from Bloody Mary. So once I got my coffee I took the opportunity in the car to make sure everything was settled for the viewings. I called the flower shop, the caterer, and the girl I used to do hair and makeup, checking to make sure everyone was running on schedule. Everything had to be finished before noon in case there were early visitors that couldn't make it to the evening viewing.

I'd gotten lucky this semester with a couple of very competent interns that I could trust to come in and make sure everything went smoothly if I wasn't there. Technically they were supposed to be interning with me for the coroner side of things, but King George wasn't exactly overrun with suspicious deaths, so the funeral home at least kept them busy while they were there.

"I didn't realize Downton Academy was so far away. Why did the Connellis live in King George if their children were going to school in McClean?"

"Downton is a boarding school, so all students live on campus. The school has a short break in the spring that started last Friday and ends today, so students can prepare for big projects and presentations that are due on Friday and also study for exams which start next week.

"I got some interesting news from Lewis when I read the update this morning. The Connellis bought the house in King George because Anthony had been receiving threats after he got the job at the Department of Defense. He's a contract engineer with high-level security clearance and he makes frequent trips to Afghanistan, so my guess is his specialty is weapons."

My brows rose. "That is interesting news."

"Connelli was a West Point graduate—computer science—and spent twelve years in the Marines, retiring as a Lieutenant Colonel. Came from a blue-collar family but worked his way up. He's well respected and there are whispers that he'd planned to run for a Senate seat in four more years. His wife was a teacher before they married, so their party thought they'd look better to the middle class."

"Gotta love politicians. I guess if she'd been a stripper they'd have figured out a way to make that work too."

Jack swerved in between cars, his hand relaxed over the wheel, never slowing his speed or losing his focus.

"The threats started about eight years ago just after he started the private contracting for the government. Private contracting is a competitive field, and a guy named Wayne Macerne got bumped when Connelli was brought in. He accused that Connelli had bought his way into the position by agreeing to overlook some weapons that had gone missing and ended up in the wrong countries. It was better that those weapons had never existed at all instead of the American people finding out and stirring up a shit storm.

"Macerne was pissed and tried to go to the media, but they shut him down. His car was run off the road one night and Macerne was banged up pretty bad—lots of broken bones, some internal injuries, and a concussion. They never caught who ran him off and he claimed over and over again that he never saw the car coming and couldn't describe it to officials.

"He was out of work about six months of recovery time. Lost the contracts he'd kept, his house and his wife. And then he got pissed and decided Connelli was to blame for all of it.

"The Connellis' home was broken into on several occasions, his office was ransacked each time. Anthony Connelli reported on more than one occasion that he was being followed, but the car was always different and he couldn't make out features on the person inside the car. Things went on like that for almost a year, Macerne was brilliant at covering his tracks.

"Macerne escalated again and started sending pictures of the kids and wife to Connelli. And then one afternoon Julia Connelli was run off the road while driving the kids home from school. They decided enough was enough, so they packed up and bought the Marcello House under a different name and basically went into hiding. Then they amped up the security system by about a thousand percent. No reported problems since they made the move."

"Scary," I said. "Where's Macerne now?"

"A tax-paying member of society. Works for a big firm in Manhattan as a lower level executive."

"I guess the DOD connection is why Cal is stuck at the scene this morning," I said.

"Good guess. They're going to be out in full mass with their own investigators, making sure there's nothing floating around the ashes that could compromise national security."

"That'll be fun. I love working with the government."

"I'm sensing sarcasm in that statement."

"I always said you were sharp as a tack." I tucked my leg under me and turned in the seat to face Jack. I knew why he was telling me about the threat. "You want me to keep checking for signs of foul play."

"Especially Anthony Connelli. I know you would anyway, but I wanted you to be aware that the DOD might be breathing down your neck for you to find something concrete."

"I can only give them what the evidence tells me. But I'll be extra thorough."

The Owens lived in a gated community in a swanky area of Alexandria. It was a place where part-time politicians had homes that they only lived in when in session. A security guard greeted us at the gate and Jack showed him his badge and told him where we were going.

The gates opened and we followed a winding road between houses that were close to the size of a city block. The lots were oversized and heavily treed, each of them having their own entry gates, which in my mind was a bit of overkill. Though with the amount of politicians in the neighborhood, maybe overkill was a necessity.

The Owens house was at the end of the street, and Jack pulled his cruiser into the driveway, stopping just shy of the iron gates and pressing the intercom button.

"Sheriff Lawson to see Dr. and Mrs. Owens," Jack said to whoever answered the intercom.

There was no reply, but the gates opened soundlessly so Jack could drive through.

"Good Lord, could they have made a longer driveway?"

"It'd be good for skateboarding with the way it slants like that."

I snorted out a laugh. "I'm sure the Owens are big skateboarders. What's he a doctor of anyway?"

"Plastic surgeon. And apparently his wife is a patient. Don't stare too hard."

With that bombshell he turned off the car and got out, leaving me inside with my mouth gaping open. I hated when he did stuff like that. Now I'd spend the whole time staring at Mrs. Owens, wondering what had been done to her.

Jack came around and opened my car door,

and I slid the autopsy report out of my bag. Just in case my word wasn't good enough and they needed to see the results with their own eyes.

The front door opened before we'd reached it and a couple stood arm in arm, their faces ashen with worry and grief. Dr. Owens was a small man, only a couple of inches taller than me, and naturally thin. His features were handsome, but his skin sagged, especially under his eyes and along his jowls, detracting from his looks. I wondered why he didn't have a colleague do some nipping and tucking, but maybe that was considered bad form.

Mrs. Owens was a couple of inches taller than her husband, super model thin, and was one of the palest people I'd ever seen in my life. I wasn't sure what milkweed was, but I'd always heard the expression about women that had skin the color of milkweed. I figured it was a description probably invented for women like Mrs. Owens. Her hair was white-blonde and her brows perfectly arched and just a shade darker. It was like looking into the sun. I had the sudden urge to put on my sunglasses.

And maybe I was staring a little longer than I should have. She didn't look to be a day over twenty-five, which either made her blessed by the heavens or her husband one of the best plastic surgeons on earth.

They knew why we were there without either of us having to say a word, and Mrs. Owens began to sob softly, her hands covering her mouth as she turned into her husband's embrace for comfort.

"Can we come inside?" Jack asked, his voice somber.

Dr. Owens nodded, his movements jerky as he tried to figure out how to move his wife out of the way and let us inside, as if his brain and hands and feet were no longer communicating with each other.

Jack put his hand at the small of my back and led me inside a spacious foyer. A double staircase led to the upper levels was the focal point, and light shone in from all the windows, glinting off the chandelier that hung from above.

I noticed my surroundings, because I'd spent enough time around Jack over the years that it had gotten to be a habit, and I cataloged everything quickly in my mind and then put it away. Just in case. But it was hard to take my eyes off Mrs. Owens. Both as a doctor and as a human being.

Her grief weighed heavily, so it was a living,

breathing thing. And the sobs she cried came from somewhere deep inside of her. Somewhere none of us would ever be able to reach. It was a purge she'd have to deal with on her own. I knew well that stage of grief, when it consumed you to the point you weren't sure you'd ever be able to crawl out and see daylight again. I didn't want to tell her, but I knew it would get worse before it got better.

Dr. Owens led us into a little sitting area off the foyer and he settled his wife down on the couch, tucking her against him like he might a child. Jack and I took the opposite facing sofa, and I knew there was no use delaying the inevitable. Quicker was better. Like a Band-Aid.

I let Jack take the lead, and his voice was soft and gentle as he said, "I'm sorry to inform you, but the remains we found at the Connelli home yesterday were identified as Cassandra."

Mrs. Owens let out a moan that made chills raise on my arms and she clutched at her stomach and bent over. I looked around the room and noticed some bottles of water tucked into the shelf of a credenza against the wall and I got up without asking to get one.

Her color wasn't good and she was having

trouble catching her breath. Dr. Owens wasn't much better off. His face had gone pale and slow tears leaked from the corners of his eyes. He was paralyzed with shock, unable to offer comfort of help.

"Mrs. Owens," I said after I'd gotten the water and unscrewed the top. I sat on the edge of the coffee table in front of her and got close, trying to make myself her focus instead of the emotions raging inside of her.

"Mrs. Owens. I want you to take long, slow breaths for me. Nice and easy." I put my hand on her wrist and felt her racing pulse flutter beneath my fingers. My voice was calm and level. "My name is Doctor Graves. You can't help us help Cassandra if you make yourself sick."

I kept talking to her, words of nonsense meant only to soothe. I wasn't sure how long we sat there before she began to do as I asked and take slower breaths, but there was an ache in my lower back.

"That's it," I said. "Can you drink some water for me?" I wrapped her hands around the bottle and made sure she could hold it steady before letting go.

"You said we can help Cassandra," Dr. Owens said, surprising me. I'd forgotten he was even there he'd been so still through the whole ordeal. His voice hitched, but he managed to hold it together. "How can we help her if she's—gone?"

"The cause of the fire is still under investigation," Jack said. "You can paint a picture for us. A timeline. We want to make sure we do right by Cassandra and the Connellis. They deserve the truth to be told, whatever it may be."

Dr. Owens nodded, and I could tell he was starting to pull himself together. The color had come back into his cheeks and his eyes were focused and determined. He had a task to do now, a way to help, and that would help him get through this interview.

"You said you were a doctor," he said. "But I didn't catch of what."

I knew this test. It was something other doctors did to measure qualifications and see exactly where you stood on the medical hierarchy. "I worked ER at Augusta General for several years before moving back home. But now I'm the coroner for King George County."

He nodded and I could tell by looking at him that he wasn't impressed. I wasn't a specialist, so that knocked me down a peg from the start. I was also a woman, and there were still a lot of male doctors, who could be some of the most chauvinistic people on the planet, who thought women had no place in medicine. My third infraction was that I was a dead doctor. No one in the medical profession had any respect for those who served the dead.

Cal had been right about how much I'd hated my time working at the hospital. I'd had to deal with bullshit like this on a daily basis. Still, he deserved to know that I'd take good care of his daughter so I told him so.

"She's our only child," he said. It was always harder to watch the men break.

"I'm very sorry for your loss." He nodded and I checked Mrs. Owens' pulse once more, satisfied it was back to normal, and then I moved back to the couch with Jack.

"Can you walk us through the last day you saw Cassandra?" Jack asked.

"We told the other detective already," Dr. Owens said. "Detective Lewis."

"I know. Just go through it again for me."

"Cassie was home for break. This is her senior year, and each of the seniors have a big presentation they have to give, both as individuals and in groups so they get the teamwork experience. The presentation counts for more than half of their grade and is a graduation requirement, so the kids spend a lot of time preparing."

"Who did Cassie team up with?"

He sighed, a small smile touching his lips. "Damian Connelli and Michael Bruce. The three of them have been inseparable for years. Damian and Michael had been best friends since grade school, and then when we moved to the area they swept Cassie along like she'd they'd been friends all their lives. And then there was little Rose, always trailing behind and wanting to be part of the group. To give Damian credit, there aren't many big brothers who would let their sisters tag along like he did.

" Those boys are like sons to us, and Cassie was like a daughter to their parents. And all three of them smart as can be. They were at the top of their class—one, two, and three. All of them had bright futures."

It didn't escape my notice how Dr. Owens kept switching between past and present tense when talking about his daughter. It would take time to adjust to her being gone.

"When did Cassie and Damian become romantically involved?"

He closed his eyes and looked up, as if asking for guidance from a higher power, and a tear slipped from beneath his lashes and ran down his cheek. "About the middle of last year. I guess they just finally noticed each other in that way and that was that. They were good kids. Great kids."

"Was it normal for Cassie to sleep over at the Connelli's? Did she know her way around the house well enough that she was comfortable?"

"Sure," he said, blowing out a breath. "She practically grew up in that house. Just like the boys are familiar with this house. Hell, they each have a bedroom upstairs if they need to stay during breaks or school holidays.

"We, the parents I mean, kind of rotate going on adult trips without the kids. Helen and I went to Paris for New Year's and Cassie stayed with the Connellis. Anthony and Julia went to Australia for three weeks last summer and Damian stayed here. So yeah, she stayed enough where she'd be comfortable in the house. Same thing for Michael. Have you found Michael? He was staying there with them. They were all working on their presentation."

"We've been unable to locate him at this time."

"John and Cherise must be beside themselves with worry."

Neither of us mentioned that no one had gotten a hold of John and Cherise Bruce. The moment one of the Senator's staff was notified, we'd have a media storm of epic proportions to deal with.

"I can only pray he's okay." He breathed out a broken sigh. "Isn't it funny how something like this makes a man pray? I've never done it before. But it just seems right somehow." He hugged his wife closer and kissed the top of her head. "I wouldn't wish this pain on my worst enemy. When can we have Cassie?"

"I should be able to release her later this afternoon, but it could be as late as tomorrow. If you'll call and tell me who you'd like to handle her interment, then I'll have her transferred as soon as I can." I handed Dr. Owens one of my cards and he studied it, running his finger along the edge.

"Thank you for taking care of her." He couldn't look me in the eyes as he said it, but I heard the sincerity and emotion behind it. Helen began to cry again, soft tears of desperation and hopelessness.

Jack and I got up and made the gesture for them to stay seated, and we saw ourselves out. I sucked in a deep breath of fresh air once we were back outside and tilted my face up to feel the sun.

"We need to find Michael Bruce," I said.

Jack's phone buzzed, and he read the text. "Ask and ye shall receive. Michael and his parents are waiting for us back at the station."

CHAPTER NINE

I called Cal on our way back to the Sheriff's Office to give him an update.

"Doctor Graves," he said. "I was just thinking about you." I could hear the smile in his voice, but also a weariness.

"Just letting you know I'm running late."

"Oh, me too. The Department of Defense is becoming a permanent pain in my ass."

"You used to tell me that. I'm glad someone else has graduated to that spot."

He barked out a laugh. "Thanks, I needed that. Lewis and Martinez are here with me. I don't know if Jack's checked his email, but they dug up an interesting bit of information about Julie Connelli."

"Oh, yeah?" I asked. I looked at Jack and

noticed he'd zeroed in on the conversation at the change in my voice. "What's so interesting?"

"She was a mail order bride. Anthony bought her from auction when she was seventeen years old. Her family needed the money bad because they were into it with the mafia."

"Holy shit."

"Pretty much. Anthony Connelli was thirty-four at the time and already making a name for himself in military circles and with intelligence operations."

"Then why would he need to buy a wife?"

"I don't know if you've seen a picture of Anthony Connelli, but that should explain it all. He was all brains. Not beauty. And word is that he was socially awkward as well. He needed a beautiful wife who could be trained up and make him look good in political circles.

"Lewis said her background check didn't expose it at first because when she came to the states Anthony paid off a judge for citizenship and a new identity—name, social security, age, birthday, and background—the works. And then Connelli put her into a finishing school of sorts so she could learn the language and lose her accent, as well as other etiquette type things."

"If he paid to have her background erased then how did it come up?" We were stuck in traffic and Jack was on his phone, no doubt reading the update on what Walker was telling me.

"That's the million dollar question. Three million dollar question actually. When we started looking through financials we found Julia Connelli had a nice little side account hidden behind the name of a charitable organization she'd founded some years back. The last deposit was made a week before the fire. And can be traced back to the Russian government."

I let out a low whistle. "So you think Julia Connelli was being paid as a double agent to gather information her husband was working on? What does the DOD think about that?"

"The DOD isn't saying much, but they're going through every scrap of debris at the scene. Lewis told me the Bruces are waiting at the police station, so at least we don't have to worry about finding him anymore.

"The DOD has given me twenty-four hours to turn over all evidence that I collected, along with a lot of threats that end with me in prison if I don't comply."

"They're a friendly lot," I said. "What are

you going to do?

"I'm going to get my ass to work on that coffeemaker and see if I can come up with a cause for the start of the fire. And then I'm going to turn everything over about a second before my twenty-four hours is up. I just escaped the DOD's watch and am headed back to get started."

"Julia Connelli is going to be first up. I'll text you when we're done at the station."

"10-4, Doc. Let me know when you're close. I'll meet you there, he said, hanging up the phone.

Jack's patience for stand still traffic had come to an end and he flipped on his lights and sirens, moving to the shoulder so he could speed past the traffic.

"Mail order bride," Jack said, shaking his head. "I tell you what, this job is never boring.

"That's the damned truth. I need to get my hands on Julia Connelli. Sometimes the dead have more information to give than the living."

The station was located just off the Towne Square. It was a long rectangular building with industrial grade red brick and ugly windows. It was attached to the courthouse, which was one of the most beautiful and ornate buildings in the area, so it made the starkness of the Sheriff's Office stand out even more.

Jack parked in the spot marked *Sheriff*, and I got out, stretching after the long ride. I waited as Jack typed in the code to the side door that entered directly into the squad room and then he ushered me back straight to his office through a back door I hadn't even known was there until a couple of months ago.

Jack's office sat to one side of the station— glass on all three sides so people could see in and he could see out. He wanted to be accessible to his men and them be accessible to him. And on the rare occasion he needed privacy, he just lowered the blinds. There was also a small, closet-sized room at the back of his office with a cot and a bathroom in case he needed to crash for whatever reason.

I could see the Bruces sitting in a secluded area off to the side, and I observed them while Jack used the intercom to speak to his secretary so she could show them back. Senator Bruce was on his phone, and I had to give him props for being involved enough with his kid to show up for something like this.

He looked like the very definition of a

politician, like they'd been all cut from the same Ken doll mold—sculpted good looks, dark hair that was silvered at the temples, a charcoal suit that could be pawned and feed a family of four for an entire year.

Mrs. Bruce was his match. Her mink colored hair was pulled back in a loose chignon, her makeup subtle, and she was wearing a pale blue pants suit that made me think of this incredible frosting Jack had made to go on the sugar cookies one Christmas. She looked ready to do battle, and after looking at her son I could see why. Mrs. Bruce was in full on protective mode.

Michael Bruce was a wreck. He was a seventeen-year-old kid who'd lost both of his best friends in a horrific way. He'd probably been one of the last people to see them alive, and that survivor's guilt would weigh on him for a long time.

He was the spitting image of his mother, but he had a polish about him you didn't find in most kids his age. He wore khakis and a striped button down shirt under a gray sweater. But that's where the polished stopped. He was slumped over in his chair, his body shaking as he wept into his hands. His mother sat with her arm around him, trying to soothe as best she could, but I could see the grief in her eyes too.

"What do you think?" Jack asked.

"They're hurting. All of them. Even the Senator, though he's trying to keep himself occupied with work."

"The mom's going to be a pain in the ass." He sighed and rubbed his hand over the top of his head in a gesture I recognized. "She's ready for battle."

We watched as Jack's secretary came to get the Bruces and lead them to his office. Betsy Clement had been the secretary for the Sheriff's Office for more than forty years. Her steel gray hair was curled in sausage rolls across her scalp and her glasses hung from a chain around her neck. She wore flower print dresses and a sweater every day, and one of her knee-hi pantyhose always ended up around her ankle by the end of the day.

She'd outlasted a lot of Sheriffs, and she knew everything. And by everything, I mean *everything*. And she'd take those secrets to her grave.

The problem with Betsy was she might be loyal and very discreet, but other than that she was a pretty awful secretary. Her memory wasn't as good as it used to be, and she and technology didn't really work so well together. So sending emails, faxes, or texts wasn't really an option. Neither was using the copy machine or the complicated phone system that connected people to different departments. And Jack was better off filling out and keeping track of his own calendar. He was counting down the days until she retired at the end of the year. I was mostly sad she wouldn't be bringing delicious brownies into the squad room once she was gone.

Jack held open the door for the Bruces to file in and showed them to the sitting area over by the window instead of the hard chairs in front of his desk. I took a seat next to him and waited.

"I'm Sheriff Lawson and this is Doctor Graves," he said, nodding at me. "Let me start off by saying that I'm very glad to see you sitting alive and well in front of me."

Michael looked at Jack with tear-drenched eyes and my heart broke for him. Just a kid who was about to grow up much too fast. "But they're not," he said, his voice choking on a sob. "Damian and Cass. They're not alive and well."

"No," Jack said softly. "I'm very sorry for your loss. For all of you." He looked up to encompass the parents and I could see that Mrs. Bruce had dropped her guard a bit because of what Jack had said.

"They were like our own children," Mrs. Bruce said, her own eyes damp, though she was trying hard to blink back the tears. "And Julia—" she couldn't hold back the tears any longer and the Senator put his hand on her shoulder in support. "Julia was one of my closest friends. I can't even begin to describe what went through our minds when we heard about the fire. We thought Michael—" her face crumpled and she took a tissue out of her purse.

"This is a very difficult time for us," the Senator said. He cleared his throat, but his voice was still raspy with emotion. "You understand our position. I don't live a private life. Cherise and I were at a fundraiser the night it happened, and we knew Michael was fine on his own. He's seventeen and about to graduate. And he's responsible. We were out late that night and then we decided to take the next day off. We do that from time to time when life gets crazy, we'll turn the phones and computers off and just disappear to spend the day with each other. And that whole time Michael could have been dead and we wouldn't have known."

"I can't believe it," Michael said, pressing his fingers to his eyes. "I still can't believe it's true. They can't be gone."

"I know this is hard for you Michael, but I'd appreciate it if you could clear a couple of things up for us. We're trying to put a timeline together." Jack looked at the Senator and Mrs. Bruce and said, "Maybe you can help too."

"You know we'll do whatever we can, but we weren't there. I don't know how much we can help you," the Senator said.

"Did Anthony ever tell you about the problems he had with Wayne Macerne?" Jack asked.

The knowledge that this could be something more than an accidental house fire penetrated the Senator's grief, and his eyes hardened. "I've known Anthony for a long time, so I remember when it happened. I'm on the Senate Defense Committee. Anthony and Julia were terrified. For themselves and the children."

"He was always there," Mrs. Bruce broke in. "You could just feel it on the back of your neck. I was out with Julia several times and we'd catch a glimpse of him. Sometimes it wasn't him, sometimes it was a woman, but we figured she and Macerne knew each other. And then there was that day he ran her off the road. They were lucky to survive."

She must have realized her choice of words because her face paled and she closed her eyes. "Stupid, isn't it. To cheat death once, only to have it come back and find you again."

"The police could never prove it was him," John said. "And believe me, they tried. But they could never catch him in the act. After they were run off the road, Julia was in the hospital for a few days. That was long enough for Anthony to buy the Marcello House. He paid cash so they could move in immediately. I helped him get it put in another name so it would be harder for Macerne to find them if he started looking."

"And they never had problems with Macerne again?" Jack asked.

I saw the answer in Mrs. Bruce's eyes even as the Senator was shaking his head no.

"Mrs. Bruce?" I asked.

She shook her head and licked her lips. "It's just that—Julia mentioned she thought she'd seen Macerne during parents' weekend a couple months back. But she assured me that was the only time, and she probably just saw someone who looked similar."

"That's enough to check him out again," Jack said.

"So you think someone did this deliberately?" the Senator asked.

"I don't have sufficient evidence to make a

ruling yet," I said. It wouldn't do us any favors for me to tell them so far things were pointing to an accidental death. But we'd be in a real fix if I found evidence down the road that ruled homicide, because the chances of getting the Senator and his wife back in for questioning was slim to none. "Cases like these take time, but the more information we have from the beginning the better."

"What about you, Michael?" Jack asked. "Did you ever hear Damian or Rose mention anything about someone hanging around?"

"No, I'm not actually sure they even knew about this guy Macerne you're talking about. I know I never have. I mean, I remember the wreck. I was supposed to go home from school with them that day, but you picked me up from school early because Nana had passed away."

"I remember," Mrs. Bruce said, touching his back softly.

I looked into Mrs. Bruce's eyes and realized there were levels to her grief. For her child and for herself, but there was something else I saw there I couldn't put my finger on.

"What time did you get to the Connelli's house that day?" Jack asked.

"I was already there," he said. "I slept over since there was no school. We had a lot of work to get done on our project, so we pretty much stayed up all night. Marta made us a late breakfast the next morning."

"Marta?" I asked.

"She's the housekeeper. She's worked for them forever."

"Has anyone contacted her?" Cherise asked. "She'll be devastated. She's the sweetest woman. And very loyal."

"Did she live on the premises?" Jack asked.

"No, she had her own family home. I'm not sure where exactly. But she came in every morning like clockwork and left at five every day, unless there was a party."

Jack made a note to find out more about Marta and continued. "What did you do after breakfast?"

"We went back upstairs to work some more. Then Rose came in later and wanted to get out the dirt bikes, so we took a break and drove the golf cart to the courts on the far side of the property."

"Michael, please tell me you didn't get on one of those dirt bikes," the Senator said.

Michael winced, the guilt on his face. "I was careful."

"You know how long it takes you to heal if you get hurt," his mother said. "Look at that paper cut on your thumb. It's still bleeding through the Band-Aid. You can't take chances like that, especially with the load of classes you'll be taking in the fall."

"What time did you leave?" Jack asked, getting them back on track.

"A little before six o'clock. We'd finished everything for the group project, but I still had some work to do on my individual presentation. So I decided to head out."

"Was that the only reason you decided to leave early?"

Michael's hands gripped the armrest of the chair, but he kept eye contact with Jack. "I guess you already have an idea." He shrugged a shoulder and tried to smile, but his lips trembled as he thought of his friends. "It's just that I didn't like being a third wheel. Damian and Cass were a unit. And sometimes things felt a little awkward if I hung around too long. You know what I'm saying?"

"Sure," Jack said. "I can understand it. We tried to find you at your house all day yesterday, but no one was home. We thought for a long time we'd be finding your remains in that house too."

Michael's cheeks flushed red and it look like he wanted to squirm in his chair, but he held himself still.

"I'm sorry about that," he finally said. "I,

uh—didn't go straight home." He looked at his parents apologetically. "I didn't even know about the fire until I heard mom's messages on my phone. I'd turned it off."

"And I was frantic because of it," she said. "Where were you?"

"Mom." Exasperation tinged his voice and he looked at his dad pleadingly. "Now isn't the time to get into this."

"For heaven's sake, Michael. We told you you were not to see that girl again. Is that where you were?"

"Mom—"

"Cherise, this isn't important right now," John said.

"We were very clear about our wishes."

Cherise looked at Jack and I as if she might find allies in us, but we sat still and silent. Sometimes you found out the most interesting things when you let people keep talking.

"She's a high school drop out and looking for an easy handout. The last thing we need is for her to show up pregnant on our doorstep. And believe me, girls like that will find a way to get what they want."

"She had to drop out because she had to go to work full time." Michael looked at me and I fought the urge to squirm in my seat. The Bruces were taking awkwardness to a whole new level. "Her mom's in jail, and she's living with an aunt, but she doesn't support her and she makes her pay rent. But Kelsey got her GED and she's taking online college classes. She's smart."

"Michael—" Cherise said again.

"This is not the time or the place for this argument," John said, his voice firmer this time. "I for one am grateful to the girl. If it wasn't for her Michael would have stayed with the Connellis that night and we wouldn't be sitting here having this stupid argument, preparing to bury our best friends and their children." His voice broke toward the end of the sentence and he clamped his lips together.

"I'm sorry," he said. "I think we probably need to go home now."

"I understand," Jack said. "We appreciate you coming in to talk to us. I know it was difficult."

"We didn't want you wasting manpower looking for Michael when he was alive and well. I've cleared my calendar for the next week. We're going to spend some time with Lance and Helen. They're going to need someone during this difficult time. Cassie was their only child."

They all stood and Jack and I followed suit. "I'll show you through the back way," he said, leading them through the private door that led back to the parking area.

When he came back in a few minutes later he came over and sat on the edge of his desk and crossed his arms over his chest.

"I need a ride to the funeral home," I said. "I'm running behind. I can get a deputy to drop me if you need to stay here."

"I'll take you." He grabbed his keys, but stopped just short of the door. "So what did you come away with just now?"

Jack liked to ask my opinion on people. I didn't like people in general, and I almost always preferred solitude over wasting my time with acquaintances who just liked to hear themselves talk instead of genuinely caring about who they were with, but it turned out my introvertedness made me a good observer and pretty accurate on the bullshit meter.

"Something is going on with the wife," I said. "I'm not sure what, but I don't think it would hurt to dig a little deeper."

"That'll be fun. Getting into the personal records of a Senator and his wife won't throw up any red flags at all."

"I worry about the increase in your sarcasm level. I feel like I've become a bad influence."

"Only in the best ways possible," he said, winking. "I can tell you right now if we request a warrant to start digging into the Bruces' records that they'll have us tied up in red tape for months and probably slap us with a lawsuit as well."

"What's the point of having a friend in the FBI if he can't help you get around all that red tape?"

Jack rolled his eyes and his lips twitched. "Ben is my best man. It's considered in bad taste to ask him to do something illegal before the wedding."

Ben Carver was one of Jack's best friends, and he'd become a good friend of mine over the past months as well. I had no idea what exactly Ben did for the FBI. I know he was in charge of a lot of people and that he was brilliant with technology.

"That's okay. I don't mind asking him," I said, shrugging. "We have two day to shut this thing down before the wedding. I'm not above begging."

"Why, Doctor Graves. One would think you almost wanted to get married."

"It'd be a shame to spend your honeymoon sleeping on the couch."

"Tough words. If there wasn't a department full of people looking in my windows right now I'd show you exactly what I can do on a couch."

He opened the door for me and smacked me on the behind playfully. "So what are you going to do about the Bruces?"

"I'll have Lewis run a cursory background check, nothing that'll raise flags, and we'll go from there. The Senator's calendar is fairly well known. That's one thing I can be thankful to the media for. Until then, maybe we'll get lucky."

CHAPTER TEN

Jack dropped me at the funeral home and gave me a quick kiss goodbye. I'd already texted Cal and let him know I was ready to roll, and he was supposed to meet me as soon as he could get free.

I let myself into the side door and closed and locked it behind me. This side of the house was closed off to the general public because I never wanted to be in a situation where people questioned the security of their loved ones. That didn't mean my security was infallible.

"Jesus, Dad," I gasped, my hand covering my racing heart. "You've got to stop doing that."

I got my phone out and started to dial Jack.

My dad was a fugitive, even though no one knew it but me and Jack. And enough was enough. He kept popping in and out of my life, screwing things up just as I was starting to feel comfortable and make decisions that were completely mine—not decisions dictated by the circumstances my parents had put me in.

"Don't call him, honey. Just give me a couple of minutes. It's important."

He looked tired. And worried. I guess being on the run wasn't all it was cracked up to be. He was a handsome man. A little under six feet in height. His body was lanky and his complexion ruddy. I'd always wondered why I hadn't inherited the beautiful color of his hair. It was like a deer pelt—a mix of reds and browns and golds that no salon could reproduce. Since I wasn't actually his kid, those dreams of inheriting certain features from my parents had been wasted wishes. His eyes were hazel, but he habitually wore tortoise shell glasses so the color was hard to see.

"Sorry, Dad. You can understand I'm a little pissed, considering you broke into our home and riffled through our things."

"Technically, yes. But I was riffling for things that belonged to me. There are flash drives missing out of that box, Jaye. I need them back and I need them back now." He was tense and worried, and his color didn't look all that great. "If those flash drives get into the wrong hands, everything I've done will have been for nothing. Your mother's death will have been in vain."

I couldn't trust him. He'd lied to me my entire life. But there was still that small part of me that wondered if he was telling the truth. If maybe all the wrongs he'd done had been for a greater right.

We stared at each other in silence for several seconds. And then I said, "I don't know what you're talking about. Maybe you just need to look again."

His lips pursed together and he looked at me with disappointment—something a child never wants to see from their parent, no matter how old. "Maybe so."

There was a knock at the kitchen door and I jumped, annoyed at myself for being caught off guard twice in a matter of minutes. I didn't have time to deal with my dad. Not with so many victims waiting.

I turned and opened the door, letting Cal in, and by the time I turned back my dad was gone. I don't know how he did it, but he was like a ghost, slipping in and out of my life with ease. He'd be back. I had something he wanted.

"Woman, you look like you've seen a ghost."

I tried to smile and shook myself out of the stupor. "Sorry. I just got here myself. I'm about to put on a pot of coffee if you want some."

"There are two things I'll never turn down in this life," he said, grinning. "One of them is coffee."

I snorted out a laugh and went over to the coffeemaker, glad I had something to do to keep my hands busy so he didn't see them shaking. Once the coffee was made I poured it into two mugs and then handed one to Cal. He liked his black, just like I did.

"You don't have any cake in the fridge, do you?"

I narrowed my eyes and took a sip of my coffee. When I was stressed or busy I had the appetite of a college sorority girl hell bent on gaining those freshmen fifteen. I'd stopped at the bakery two days ago and bought a readymade birthday cake right out of the case.

"You can have cake *after* the autopsies. No reason to waste a perfectly good cake if you end up being a weenie."

"I think I'm offended by that. I can hold

my cake."

"But not your bourbon," I said, hiding my smile in my coffee cup.

"Ouch, Doc. You've grown more teeth over the years."

"Working in the ER made me tough."

"You certainly look different. It's nice to see you without bags under your eyes and in something besides those ugly green scrubs."

"Thank you. I don't know how I would've gone on without knowing that."

Cal's smile was wide and he took his cup to the sink, running water in it. "I didn't realize we were supposed to dress up for an autopsy," he said, pointing to my clothes. "I like the purple. But that sweater isn't going to be nearly so nice with brain matter all over it."

"A little extra brain matter never hurt anyone. I just need to make sure my skull saw is spitting in your direction so you get your fair share."

He laughed out loud, a big belly laugh that made me smile. "It's good to see you, Jaye."

He squeezed my shoulder good-naturedly and I had to fight the urge to shrug it off. His touch was familiar, yet foreign, and it made me uncomfortable to remember the level of intimacy I'd shared with someone else. Jack's touch was the only one I wanted. Cal must have picked up on my discomfort because he took a step back and put his hands in his pockets while he waited for me to make the next move.

I went to the lab door and typed in the code and waited for the door to open.

"Good Lord, what is that smell?" Cal asked.

I saw him swallow a couple of times and take a step back.

"It's the embalming fluid. It permeates everything, so it settles during the time I'm not down there. It'll dissipate once I turn the fans on."

"That's inhumane. Nothing should smell like that."

"I know. Give me good old decomposition any day."

I turned the fans on and true to word, the smell disappeared. He followed me down to the basement. "I never pictured you coming back here," he said, to fill the silence. "You were always adamant about getting the hell out of Bloody Mary and forging your own path."

"Yeah, well best laid plans and all that. I didn't want to come back."

"I heard about your parents."

I snorted out a laugh. "*Everyone's* heard

about my parents. Was it the driving off a cliff in what appeared to be a double suicide that caught your attention, or the fact that they were using this funeral home to smuggle contraband inside the bodies and caskets they took in from deceased members of the military that were coming in from overseas?"

Somewhere along the way, the shock had worn away and I'd come to peace with the kind of people my parents were. Jack had helped me heal. It was an ongoing process, but every day was better. The aches more bearable and the pain less soul crushing. Which was why it was all the more important to convince my dad to stay out of my life.

Cal's lips quirked. "It was certainly an attention getter. I'm surprised Hollywood hasn't come calling wanting to tell the story."

"I'm still weighing my options. I want artistic control."

"Ha!," he said. "Jack's going to have his hands full with you."

"I certainly hope so. Otherwise, what's the point?"

I went to the freezer and stood inside the door, the frigid air chilling me to the bone in only moments. I grabbed the adult female and pulled her toward the table. Cal helped me transfer, and I gave him points for doing it without having to be asked.

I still had to identify each set of remains—even though probability told me that it was more than likely Julia Connelli—and compare dental records, because the fire had made it impossible to do a visual identification.

I suited up in my smock and apron and lab coat, fairly certain I'd protected all of my clothing, and I attached the recorder back to my lapel like I had the night before. I did a visual rundown of sex and age, also determining by the pelvic area that she'd given birth. And then I went over the body, pulling fibers and looking for distinguishing marks.

"So marriage, huh?" Cal asked when the silence dragged on too long. He'd never been one of those people who was okay with comfortable silence. Which pretty much drove me crazy, because one of the things I loved most in life was the ability for everyone around me to shut up.

I looked at Cal and arched a brow. "You seem surprised."

"You always seemed to be against marriage. I just wondered what changed your mind."

"No, that was you who was against marriage. I was just too busy with my career."

He grinned unapologetically. "Oh, right. I remember now. It was me."

I rolled my eyes and prepared the body for x-rays. "Here, put this on and stand over there," I said, handing him the lead vest.

"It's just funny to meet the man you always talked about. I pictured him differently."

"Oh, yeah?" I asked, distracted by the job I was doing instead of what Cal was saying. "How did you picture him?"

I was starting to remember what our problems had been. He felt the need to fill the silence all the time and I felt the need to block him out to maintain the silence in my head that I needed to function.

"I don't know." I could hear the shrug in his voice. "Uglier, for one."

My head snapped up at that. I thought he'd been kidding, but he was serious. "Uglier? What in the hell gave you the impression that Jack was ugly?"

"Come on, why wouldn't I think that? A dude is best friends with a girl his whole life and he doesn't make a move? He's either gay or ugly."

"I remember why we didn't work out. It's all coming back very clear."

He smiled again. "Because we would have driven each other crazy if we'd continued on as we were. Plus the whole fear of commitment thing."

I cleared away the x-ray materials and went back to the body, setting the spotlight lower and directly over the face. I wanted to look inside the mouth again.

"Hand me that scraper on the tray, would you?" I asked, holding out my hand like I had in the ER, waiting for my orders to be answered. The cold metal handle went into my glove and I pried the mouth open a little wider.

"Anyway, I guess what I'm trying to say is that it's good to see you happy. You weren't, not really, working at the hospital and being away from your family. As much as you kept telling yourself that's where you were supposed to be."

"Why have you turned into Dr. Phil in your old age? Are we going to have to hug soon and talk about our feelings?"

"Who are you calling old? I take offense to that. I'm in my prime. And my knees hardly pop at all whenever I have to walk upstairs, and I can still sleep through the night without having to get up and go to the bathroom. That's pretty good in my book." He leaned over from the other side of the body so the top of our heads almost touched. "What are you looking for?"

"I'm taking scrapings of this dental work so

I can run some tests. But this is not American dental work. I can tell that just by looking. The materials are different. And also the level of decay on some of her back teeth is indicative of a place that might not have the same quality of medical care that we do here. At least thirty or forty years ago when she had these procedures done. "

"Russian?"

"Could be. Let's match up dental and make sure this is Julia Connelli."

I put up all the x-rays on the light board and then opened the manila envelope that contained her dental x-rays.

"Well, that's certainly strange," I said, comparing the x-rays I'd taken to her medical files.

"What's that?" Cal asked.

"It looks like she's had a couple of procedures done," I said, pointing to the scar tissue under her chin that showed up white on the x-ray film. "Liposuction under the chin. She's had her cheekbones sculpted. See the scarring on the bone? A chin implant, rhinoplasty, and a breast augmentation. But there's no mention of this work in her medicals. Nothing more than a bout with pneumonia she suffered almost ten years ago, and then the births of her children, which were both cesarean sections."

"Bring her over. Change her name and her looks. He wouldn't want it to become public knowledge."

"Keeping a secret like that would be expensive. And back in those days he didn't have that kind of money. But Anthony Connelli created the perfect wife for himself."

"There ain't no such thing, Graves," Cal said, shaking his head. "Stupid man."

"You're going to have to get over this whole commitment issue you have. There are a lot of nice women out there who will put up with your bullshit. And you're getting to that age where you're going to need someone to feed you pudding and make sure your bowels are regular."

"I'll make sure to add that to my Match.com profile. I'm sure the women will be lining up at the door. Is that why you're marrying Jack? So you can have someone to take care of you in your old age? Don't think I didn't notice those two gray hairs on your head."

"I'm marrying Jack because I love him. And I don't care about having someone to take care of me in my old age. I just want to grow old with him."

"At the risk of sounding mushy, I want you

to know I really am happy for you. You're good people, J.J. Graves. You've forged your own path and you've never looked back. That's what people will remember. Not where you came from."

A lump formed in my throat and I nodded because I wasn't sure I could speak. I cleared my throat and broke eye contact, looking back at the x-rays on the light board.

"Thanks for that, Cal. It means a lot. Really." I sucked in a deep breath and held it for a few seconds. "The dental is a match," I said, moving on so I didn't break down and cry like a baby. "A confirmed match for Julia Connelli. No signs of abuse on the body. No fresh wounds. And there was smoke and burns in the airway."

"Accidental death."

"That's what it looks like," I said, biting my bottom lip.

"That's pretty much my thought too. That's what it looks like, but I don't believe in coincidences. Especially when one of them works for the DOD and the other is a Russian mail order bride. We just need to look harder."

The words had barely left his lips when I saw what might have been our first break. "What does that look like?" I asked, moving closer to the x-ray to get a better look.

"I don't know. Your head is in the way."

I moved back to let him see, pointing at the neck and wondering if I was just so tired I was manifesting things to get answers.

"It looks like a pin hole," he said. "I think."

"See how it tapers at the end once it enters the muscle?"

"Kind of. Don't laugh, but I think I need my reading glasses." He pulled out a pair of wire-framed reading glasses from his front pocket and slipped them on, staring intently at the pin hole. "Okay, that's better. I see it."

"That's a syringe mark," I said, the feeling of excitement starting to flow through me. "Jesus, I could've missed it on Cassandra Owens."

I ripped down Julia's x-rays and stacked them quickly, shoving them in an envelope and putting them aside. And then I pulled out the file I'd started for Cassandra Owens and put all of her x-rays back up. It was a shot in the dark, but like Cal said, I didn't believe in coincidences either.

"Son of a bitch," I murmured under my breath. "I missed it."

"I'm not seeing this one," Cal said.

"It pierced a major artery. It's darker on the x-ray, so not as easy to see. But there are air bubbles around it from when the plunger was pressed and the drug administered. You see?"

Three tiny air bubbles, so microscopic as to almost being invisible, but one of the most important pieces of evidence we might have.

"Yeah, I see it now." He looked at me, the fun loving and easy-going Cal gone, replaced by the veteran cop that had seen and done it all. Cops who'd lived the job and not just put on their weapon every day to sit behind a desk had a certain look about them. Cop eyes and mannerisms that were easy to recognize and impossible to decipher.

We set into motion, both of us understanding what needed to be done without having to communicate with more than the occasional grunt or wave of a hand. We wrapped up Julia Connelli and pushed her back in the freezer. I'd do the autopsy on her later. But these initial findings were the most pressing at the moment. Everyone was waiting to see whether I'd declare the scene as an accidental death or a homicide, and I had to be accurate. The Connellis and Cassandra Owens deserved justice.

One by one, we pulled each victim out of the freezer and set them up for x-rays. By the time we got to the last one, I was sweating beneath the layers of my lab coat and apron. I knew what we'd find before we put the x-rays up on the light board, side by side, each labeled to differentiate the victims. But it wasn't enough to make the call. Not yet.

I had to send DNA samples off to Richmond to be tested, and that often took weeks because of the backup in the lab, though the testing itself only took a few minutes. But I was able to do my own toxicology testing here in the lab. It saved time and money, especially in cases where we needed answers quickly.

It wasn't often I worked on multiple victims at once, and it was time consuming because I had to make sure that every scrap of evidence, every fiber, hair, blood sample or semen sample was labeled appropriately. Especially if it was going to be admissible in court at some point.

"It's a paralytic," I said, looking at the blood comparisons from each victim several hours later. "They were each injected with a drug to cause paralysis but not to kill. That's why they all had burn and smoke in the airways."

"Jesus. That's an awful way to die. Cruel."

"Specifically they administered pancuronium bromide. It's a muscle relaxer used during anesthesia." I immediately thought of Dr. Owens, and wondered if a man could sacrifice his only child for a higher agenda. There'd been worse things happen in the world.

"If I remember right, it's also a drug used during lethal injections. We could be looking at any number of people who could get their hands on a drug like that."

"Thank God that job falls to the police. All I can tell you is the how. Not the who or why."

"Lets say Julia Connelli was a double agent who was filtering classified information back home and whoever is giving her orders decided she was ineffective or her job was done. Could her dose have been self-administered? Can you tell by the angle of entry?"

"Not really. But why would she self-terminate if a large amount of money had just been deposited into her account? I'd be more likely to take it and run. She changed her identity once. She could do it again. And thanks to her husband she has the connections to do so."

"How long would the injection put them out for?"

"Around two hours. Plenty of time for the fire to start and spread. And if the coffee pot exploded like you think then that could explain why the fire spread so quickly without the use of an accelerant."

"I'm almost there reconstructing the coffee pot, so I'll have an answer soon. The alarm company notified the fire department at 12:47, and first responders said the house was completely engulfed and already collapsing when they arrived seventeen minutes later. What we have to look at is the time it took for the fire to get to that point. The alarm company would have been notified the moment smoke set off the alarms."

"And the Connellis could have been administered the drug as early as 11:00, but probably a little later just to be on the safe side. A paralytic like that affects people differently—metabolism and weight have a lot to do with how long they'd be under. Whoever used the drug wouldn't want to take the chance that they'd wake up before the smoke could kill them."

I pulled out my phone and dialed Jack. "It's homicide," I said as soon as he answered. I explained about the syringe marks and the results from the tox screen.

"I'd have been surprised if it wasn't homicide. The Connellis were fascinating people. You know who else is fascinating?"

"Doctor Owens?"

"Bingo, kid. We'll debrief as soon as you get a chance. When does Walker's twenty-four hour time period end?"

I relayed the question to Cal. "About ten o'clock tomorrow morning," he said. "But I could get stuck in traffic for a couple of hours if need be. You know how D.C. is during rush hour."

"Good to know," Jack said. "We'll stretch it for as long as we can. Just FYI, Jaye, my mother is in the lobby of the funeral home greeting people and showing them which rooms to go to."

I looked up at the clock and saw it was almost seven o'clock. I'd lost complete track of time while working on the bodies.

"Your mother?" Mrs. Lawson was an amazing woman, and she could do just about anything she set her mind to, so I wasn't worried about her handling anything upstairs. I just felt guilty that someone else was having to do the job I was supposed to be responsible for.

As if reading my mind, Jack said, "You can't do it all, Jaye. The victims take priority. You know that. And it never hurts to ask for help every now and then."

"The families of the people upstairs are

paying for my services." I started covering the bodies back up with the white sterile sheets, and then Cal pushed them back into the freezer while I stripped out of my apron and lab coat.

"They're paying for the services of Graves Funeral Home. It's a family business. And if my mother hasn't been your family for most of your life I don't know who has."

"Right. Text her and tell her I'll be there as soon as I can. I need to freshen up so I don't look like a corpse. And tell her not to let Rosalyn Harrison get too close to the casket in viewing room three. She's the deceased's most recent ex-wife and she likes her gin more than she did her husband. She'll end up in the casket with him if no one is watching."

"Mom will like that. You know how bored she's gotten since she retired."

"Your mom is never bored. She's on a dozen committees and knows everything that happens in this town before you do. Give her a little credit."

"Don't give her too much," Jack said, laughter in his voice. "She's probably hoping Rosalyn ends up in that casket. Otherwise she won't have anything to talk about at her bridge game tomorrow."

"Sure she will. We're getting married in two

days. That should give her enough to talk about for the next couple of years. But just in case, I'll hurry."

CHAPTER ELEVEN

It was after ten o'clock by the time I got everyone out of the funeral home. That included Jack and Cal after quite a bit of protest from both sides, but at least I was able to convince Jack to bring my Suburban from the house and leave it in the driveway so I'd have a way to get back home.

We had plans to debrief the following morning, and I knew they would be getting as much sleep as I would. I need eight solid hours alone with my bodies to finish the autopsies. The evidence the bodies gave me was like a puzzle that only I could sort from my end. The evidence collected on Jack and Cal's end was the same—the timelines and stories of people's lives, never quite as honest as they'd like you to believe—coming together to paint the complete picture.

According to Jack, Anthony Connelli had one brother, and he was the closest living relative to claim the remains once I'd finished the autopsies. I'd be shipping the Connellis to a crematorium in D.C. and Cassandra Owens to a funeral home her parents had selected. It took weight off my shoulders to not have to keep them there and deal with the services. The media frenzy by itself would be a mess. I'd had several local reporters try to sneak in as mourners during the viewings earlier so they could get the scoop on the Connellis. Mrs. Lawson had been especially happy to show them to the door.

Years of working twenty-four hour shifts made nights like this one more bearable. My brain remembered the grueling pace automatically and went into that mode that shut off everything else—all bodily discomforts—and allowed me to focus on nothing but the job.

There were no windows in the lab, so I missed the sunrise as I slid the last body back inside the freezer and made a few final notes. There would be time for me to notice the exhaustion later. Or maybe not. My phone alarm beeped, reminding me we had the rehearsal dinner that evening. Apparently that was something I had to be presentable for.

It was just past six-thirty when I made the drive home and parked next to Jack's cruiser. He had a black truck he kept in the garage and drove when he wasn't on duty, which didn't seem to be very often.

The smell of something amazing greeted me as I came inside and I headed straight for the kitchen, thinking if I could get another pot of coffee in me I might make it through the whole rehearsal thing without falling asleep in my soup. Or whatever we were having. I was assuming that was one of the details Vaughn and Mrs. Lawson had seen to.

I was surprised to find Cal in the kitchen with Jack when I came in. I grunted to both of them and took the cup of coffee Jack held out at me. They both still wore the same clothes as they had from the night before.

"Anything interesting on your end?" Jack asked.

"Just your good old garden variety murder victims. The little girl, Rose, had Crohn's disease. Anthony had a pretty serious blockage in his heart that would've needed to be seen to pretty quick had he lived. Damian was a healthy seventeen year old kid. And Julia Connelli was your basic Russian

Frankenstein's monster. I'm not sure there was any part of her that was real. In this case, the autopsies didn't tell us anything we didn't already know."

"You releasing them to the families?" Cal asked.

"They'll be transported this afternoon. I've got a funeral at eleven o'clock and another at three, so I'm keeping my fingers crossed the timeline works out. I need to clone myself."

"Let's not get carried away, sweetheart," Jack said. "I can barely keep up with one of you. Now eat your bacon. The protein is good for you."

"You know, I'm a doctor. I know exactly what the bacon is doing to the inside of my body. But it is delicious and I'm going to eat it anyway. I also want one of those cinnamon rolls I smell in the oven."

"You've got a nose like a K-9."

Jack wasn't just an average cook. He was an exceptional cook, and he seemed to enjoy it. And believe me, it didn't detract from his alpha status one bit. Watching him in the kitchen was one of the sexiest things I'd ever seen. He pulled out two trays of cinnamon rolls and divided them up to place on a tray.

"Jesus, I'm going to weigh three hundred pounds by the time I'm done with this case,"

Cal said. "But it would be rude not to eat one."

I snickered and grabbed at a gooey bun. "You don't have to worry about the whole cloning thing," I told Jack. "My interns are going to pinch hit for me during the funerals today. I've got enough on my plate with getting the bodies transferred. And I don't suppose you know anything about all this wedding shit that magically popped up on my calendar for today? I think Vaughn keeps adding things just to fuck with me."

"I wouldn't put it past him. What kind of wedding stuff?"

"Girl stuff. Manicure and pedicure. Some kind of hair treatment that I'm already dreading. I'm assuming you're not being held to the same kind of torture?"

"No. I just have to show up and get married. You should try that."

"Don't tell Vaughn, but I'm pretty sure I'm going to have a technology glitch and delete those appointments from my calendar. You like my fingers and toes like they are, right?"

"Is this one of those trick questions that can have no right answer?" Jack asked.

"Only if you answer wrong." I realized my plate was empty and took it to the sink. "What about you guys? What's new on the law and order side of things?"

"We started setting up the boards last night. Lewis will be back in a little bit. He left to shower and change clothes. You know how he is. And Martinez is upstairs catching some shut eye."

"He said he needed his beauty sleep for the wedding tomorrow," Cal said. "Weddings are prime territory for picking up the ladies."

Jack rolled his eyes. "Not to mention the fact that Martinez turns into a real bitch when he doesn't get regular sleep or meals. Good thing he's not a cop in a bigger city."

I followed the guys into the front living area across from the kitchen. It had been turned into an office of sorts over the last few months. Gone was the comfortable furniture that had once been placed in front of the fireplace, and in its place was a long wooden table and walls of white boards with extra markers and magnets so we could rearrange things quickly if we needed to.

They'd gotten a good start on setting things up. On the center white board were pictures of the Connelli family in a straight line across the top. Next to them was a picture of Cassandra Owens. Below their smiling images were pictures of each body from the fire scene. It was always important to never forget the victim. And to have those faces staring at us kept everyone motivated to find justice.

On the white board to the left of the victims was a picture of Wayne Macerne. I wasn't sure what he did at the firm he worked for in Manhattan, but just looking at his picture gave me chills. The look in his eyes didn't inspire trust.

On the white board on the right side was a different set of pictures. Lance and Helen Owens and John and Cherise Bruce. And next to them was a picture of Michael Bruce.

"Who's this?" I asked, pointing to the unfamiliar female next to Michael.

"Kelsey Donaldson is her name. She's Michael's girlfriend. Lewis tracked her down yesterday afternoon. She waits tables at a restaurant near the capitol building, but she lives with an aunt in Fredericksburg. A rough neighborhood, according to Lewis. Rough enough that he didn't stop at the aunt's house, but waited to catch Kelsey at work. It would have caused problems if people in that neighborhood had seen them talking to the cops."

"I can't see a Senator's kid shacking up in a neighborhood like that, even for the sex."

"He's not stupid," Jack said, nodding. "He's got a bottomless trust fund and access to the money, so he reserves a hotel room at the Marriott downtown. He stays there often enough that the staff recognized him, but he and Kelsey never enter or leave together.

"Kelsey said Michael was already at the hotel waiting for her when she got there at seven. She said they ordered room service and didn't leave until Michael got the call from his parents the next afternoon. Lewis said she seemed like a sweet kid. She's a couple years older than Michael but has a head on her shoulders."

"Any luck tracking down Wayne Macerne?" I asked.

"I called a friend with NYPD and he did some legwork for us. According to his employer, Macerne's been at work every day this week, arriving about twenty till eight and leaving right at six o'clock in the evening. There's no record of him leaving the state. No purchases on his credit cards or debit card for anything outside the state. He's got a small house in Brooklyn. My buddy says his neighbors describe him as quiet and staying to himself. He never has company that they've noticed."

"That doesn't mean he couldn't have made the drive. It's a five hour drive from Manhattan to here. That would put him at the

Connelli's house right at eleven o'clock or a little after if he left work at six. Plenty of time for him to break in and administer the drug. And he's an engineer. He'd have the skills to bypass their security system and rig the coffee pot to start the fire."

"Speaking of the coffee pot," Cal said. "I was able to finish the reconstruction."

I'd completely missed the little table in the corner where pieces of the coffee pot were laid out. It looked like a mess to me, but to Cal it was something completely different.

"The protective coating around the coils was removed. There's a maximum temperature they're allowed to reach in order to be sold to the public, but without those protective coatings the coils get hot enough to melt anything they touch. There was no evidence that coffee had been prepared, which meant he set it to run dry. The way the coffee maker was placed under the kitchen cabinets, as soon as it got hot enough to catch fire, those cabinets were perfect tinder.

"The house was old and they'd used as much of the original craftsmanship as possible. The wood of the cabinets was old, and when you combine it with the lead paint that was still part of the wood, the whole thing would've spread very quickly. Under normal circumstances, it would've been a good way to commit the crime. If he'd set the timer of the coffee maker to where it went off in the middle of the night, there wouldn't have been sufficient evidence for you to declare it a homicide. But he made a mistake administering the drug."

"Which begs the question, where'd he get the drug? And how are we going to prove he did it?" I said.

"If we can find substantial evidence to tie him to the crime, we'll get him. There was blood on the coil. It looks like when he stripped off the coating he pricked his finger. Fire doesn't destroy DNA."

I looked at the enormity of this case and felt frustration well up inside me. Normally I was invigorated by the process of bringing victims justice. But I was tired. We'd just come off a big case less than two weeks before, and truth be told, I was still shaken up by it. I'd come way too close to losing Jack. And now we were staring down what seemed to be an impossible case, with more red tape and wrong turns than we could ever hope to weave through. All I wanted was to get married and take a small break. But looking at the victims' faces in front of me, I wasn't sure that was going to happen.

"Jaye," Jack said. "We're getting married tomorrow. This case doesn't live and die by us, as much as it may feel like. They can solve this case without us."

"Right," I agreed.

Though it felt like we were quitting, and that didn't settle too well with me. But I knew Jack was right. We deserved a personal life. And as much as both of us entrenched ourselves in work, it was sometimes hard to remember to take time out for ourselves and make sure we were nourishing the personal relationship as well as the professional.

Three rapid knocks sounded at the door and Jack went to let in Lewis. His hair was still damp and he was dressed down from his usual work attire. Come to think of it, I wasn't sure I'd ever seen him in jeans before.

"Anything new?" Lewis asked

"We were just catching Jaye up to speed," Cal said.

"Did you tell her about Doctor Owens?"

"Oh, yeah," I said, remembering Jack had mentioned something about it last night. My brain was starting to get foggy from lack of sleep. "What did you find?"

"Lance Owens and Anthony Connelli went to high school together. They attended different colleges, but were roommates up in

Boston until Lance started medical school and moved to New York. Connelli stayed on in Boston to finish his Master's, but they stayed in touch. And it was actually Connelli who introduced Lance to his wife at a party. She was a law student at the same college Connelli attended."

"Mrs. Owens is an attorney?" I asked, trying to picture the woman I'd met yesterday in a courtroom.

"She quit her last semester when she married Lance. But she heads a lot of charitable organizations," Lewis explained.

"So Connelli and Owens grew up together. That's not really a surprise, I guess. He said they were all very close when we talked to him yesterday."

"Owens is a plastic surgeon," Jack said. "One of the best in the nation from what we understand. There's a reason all the work done on Julia Connelli never showed up in her medical reports."

"Oh," I said, the light dawning. "Sorry. My brain is sleep deprived. Owens performed the surgery. No records. And probably a hell of a discount."

"Bingo," Jack said.

"I invited him in for questioning," Lewis said. "He'll be arriving at the station in about an hour."

"If he performed the surgery then he more than likely knew where she came from," I said. "That kind of information is potential blackmail, especially if Julia was acting as a double agent on behalf of Russia."

"But what would Owens be blackmailing Connelli for?" Cal asked. "There's no motive there that I can see. The only thing Connelli has of value is the work he does for the Department of Defense. What's a plastic surgeon going to do with that?"

"Someone who could do something with that is a Senator on the Defense Committee," Jack said.

"Except our hands are tied there as far as requesting information," I said. "Were you able to find out anything from a surface look?"

"Just the basics," Jack said, rubbing his hands across the top of his head. "Bruce's father was Governor, so he came by politics naturally. Was an average student. Got his business degree from Yale. Married at twenty-eight to Cherise Whitcomb-Weiss, the daughter of former Secretary of State Edgar Weiss. Bruce is on his third term as Senator, and is fairly popular. They have two children. Their oldest daughter Charlotte is in her third year of law school. And Michael is seventeen and a senior at Downton Academy. Second in his class. He'll be attending Yale in the fall as a biochemistry major. IQ is off the charts, but has a tendency to be lazy, though he's seen quite a bit doing community work. Has a soft spot for the less fortunate.

"The Bruces were at a fundraiser like they said the night of the fire. Thanks to the Internet there's plenty of pictures to prove it. There's even one showing them leaving the event, just after midnight."

"The media are so helpful," I said. "I don't know how law enforcement survives without them."

"Funny," Jack said, straight-faced. "The bottom line is, we need to know more about the Bruces and any ties they might have to the Connellis that aren't just on the surface. With Anthony with the Department of Defense and the Senator on the Defense Committee, you know their paths cross. And they may not always cross on amicable terms. If the Senator found out the truth about Julia, there are any number of scenarios that could've played out."

"Surely Ben owes us a favor," I said.

"I'm pretty sure we owe Ben our first born child after all the favors he's done us," Jack said. "Sometimes there are ways to work around the law to get what's needed. Sometimes there's not. This is one of those times. And we might just have to face the reality that this case might not be solved any time soon. We're going to have to go through the appropriate channels and do everything by the book. Especially if there's a Senator involved."

I shook my head and looked at Jack carefully. Jack was one of the most patient men I'd ever known. I couldn't remember the last time I'd seen him lose his temper. But there was a definite bite in his words. My own hackles rose, but I knew better than to argue in front of his men. The air was definitely charged though, and the others must have sensed it.

"I'm going to go catch an hour of sleep before I have to turn evidence over to the DOD," Cal said.

Lewis put his hands on his hips and rocked back on his heels. "Yeah. I'm, uh—I'm going to grab Martinez and head into the station to prep for Doctor Owens."

Everyone scattered and left Jack and I facing each other. He was leaning against the table, his arms crossed over his chest and staring at me with disinterest in his gaze. It was an effective tactic when fighting. Aloneness and feeling isolated was a trigger point for me. I'd felt that way all my life, and Jack knew it.

When Jack got mad, he didn't argue and his voice didn't become louder. He didn't throw his hands around in frustration or pace back and forth. He shut down completely. He became indifferent.

And to me that was worse than if he did have a normal reaction. Because when he got angry he closed himself off and you didn't know what he was thinking or feeling. He was an island unto himself. His features and heart hardened, and the distance he put between himself and anyone else felt like a canyon.

I was the first to break the silence. "What the hell, Jack? This doesn't sound like you. Why are you angry?"

"I'm not angry."

I refrained from rolling my eyes at the most blatant lie I'd ever heard. "Fine. You're not angry. So what's the problem? Other than the fact that there are five victims weighing on your shoulders and you haven't slept?"

"I know we're at the forty-eight hour mark on this case and we've got nothing. And it feels like you've done nothing but pressure me to break the law so we can solve this case, and to hell with ethics or anything else."

"I beg your pardon?" I asked, my voice becoming very level, which was never a good sign. "I'm pressuring you to break the law? Really?"

"What do you think suggesting we call in Carver would be doing, Jaye?"

"A joke? And don't say my name in that tone of voice. I'm not a child to be disciplined."

"Well, you're not acting like an adult. We don't have time for this." He moved to leave the room and I stood in front of the door.

"Oh, no. You're not going to just walk away and leave me like I'm in the wrong here. I know you believe in the law above all else. I wouldn't love you the way I do if you didn't. But it's not like you to just shrug your shoulders and give up on a case before we've barely gotten started. The Connellis deserve better than that. And so does Cassandra Owens."

"You don't have to fucking remind me who the victims are. I can see their faces as well as you can."

I raised my eyebrows in surprise and felt genuine worry seep into my soul. I'd never seen Jack like this. Or heard him take that tone of voice with me.

"What is going on, Jack? This isn't you."

"I don't know. But if you'd rather see this case out to the end instead of leave on our honeymoon, just let me know."

I gasped and my body jerked back as if he'd struck me. "You've changed your mind about getting married? You don't want to?"

Somewhere deep inside of me, it's what I'd been afraid of from the beginning. Why would a man like Jack—a good and honorable man in all things—want someone like me? A girl who came from the worst of the worst. Who didn't mind bending the rules or walking in those shades of gray from time to time if it served a purpose. Jack would always do what was right, even if it was detrimental to himself.

I had a strong moral code, but it was my own definition. I believed that right should always win and that good should always prevail. But even though I was the one who'd had the kind of upbringing that exposed me to some of the darker things in life, Jack had actually lived in those dark areas. And sometimes, like now, I wondered if he'd ever really come back from it.

"Jesus, Jaye," he said, exasperated. "No, that's not what I'm saying. I'm just saying if you're so fixated on this case and finding answers then we can do whatever you want. Just let me know."

"Just let you know?" I asked, a tear escaping to fall down my cheek. "Did someone just inhabit your body in the last twenty minutes and take over? You know what my answer is to "Just let you know?" I swiped at the tear on my cheek, my breath coming in big gulps. "My answer to that is fuck you. When you decide to be honest with me and tell me what's really wrong, how about you just let *me* know."

I turned on my heel and grabbed my bag from the hall table, shutting the front door behind me softly. Jack didn't try to stop me.

CHAPTER TWELVE

I did what I always do when I was upset. I turned to the dead.

I drove to the funeral home with my eyes dry and my body numb. I couldn't think about any of it right now. Not unless I wanted to break down completely, and that wouldn't do the Connellis or Cassie Owens any good.

I was long past sleep. I'd pushed past the hard part and I'd hit my second wind, my mind vividly sharp, but my reactions almost in slow motion. I took fifteen minutes to shower and change clothes. I put on jeans and a gray Henley and my boots, and shoved my wet hair behind my ears.

I went to the kitchen to make a pot of coffee and saw Ben Carver standing outside the door. I sighed and banged my head against the cabinet twice, wondering what the chances were that he'd show up out of the blue when we'd just been talking about him. Despite my wanting to pretend I hadn't seen him and head downstairs, I went to open the door.

"I don't mean to toot my own horn," he said by way of greeting, "But that's usually not the reaction women have when they see me."

"Hello, Ben."

Ben was a couple years older than Jack, and a couple inches shy of six feet.

"Jaye. I've seen corpses that have more color than you. Heh, get it," he said, wagging his eyebrows.

"You're hilarious. I haven't been to bed yet. You should probably come inside so you don't have to tell all your lame jokes from the porch."

"I can tell you've been practicing talking to live people instead of dead ones. You're so personable." He batted his eyelashes and I almost laughed. But not quite. "Did I come at a bad time?"

"Not really. I was just about to head down to the lab. No one's here but me if you were looking for Jack. And I'm not great company at the moment."

"You're about to get married, woman.

Brides should be happy and blushing or something. Or at least getting drunk with their best friends and making questionable last minute choices."

"Hmm," I said, turning my back to go to the coffeepot. I really needed to lighten up on the coffee. I knew it wasn't healthy, but it was my crutch. I went to the fridge and added milk just to change things up, and then I pulled the cake out and set it on the counter.

"Are you really eating cake for breakfast?"

"I've already had breakfast. I'm having brunch." I sliced two squares and put them on plates. "You're having breakfast."

"I don't mean to stick my nose into your business," he said, arching an eyebrow as I handed him the cake. "I mean, yeah, I kind of do and I'm going to whether you want me to or not, but I thought it would sound better if I told you that first."

"I have no idea what you just said, but I'm getting the gist that you're going to interfere."

"Only a little. I went by the house first and Jack's looking worse than you are."

"I don't mean to be rude, but you're Jack's friend. Why did you come here?"

"See, there you go with being personable again. You remind me of my wife. She says the same thing to me a lot."

"Someday I'd like to meet this elusive wife you keep talking about. I think I'd like her."

"Oh, you would. Which is why I haven't brought her around yet. I don't need you ganging up on me." He put a bite of cake in his mouth and made a face, sticking out his tongue to wipe some of the icing off. "My God, woman. This is pure sugar. Haven't you noticed my body is a temple?"

"I don't have my glasses on."

"Good one." He scraped the icing off the cake and then started eating again. "Listen, in all seriousness, I'm not just Jack's friend. I'm yours too. I don't know what happened. And I won't ask. But I know I see two people hurting who are meant to be with each other."

I pushed the cake around on my plate a bit before finally putting it down.

"I'm going to give you some advice, without telling you too much information," Carver said. "You and Jack have been friends your whole lives, but the relationship aspect is fairly new. There are things you're going to have to be patient about.

"I've known Jack for eleven years. I knew him when he worked undercover those first few years, and I knew him when he moved to S.W.A.T. Things like that change a man. You start losing your friends—your brothers—and each death weighs a little heavier on the soul. You hide it behind smile and jokes and with different women, none of which you keep around long because you don't want to have to explain to them the nightmares or the fact that you sat in your car for twenty minutes looking at your service revolver and wondering whether you should just pull the trigger."

I felt the tears run down my face, but I didn't try to stop them. I'd seen these glimpses in Jack, and all I could do was pray that I could somehow make it better for him—ease the hurt. Because when he hurt, I hurt.

"All I'm saying is be patient. Sometimes certain events can trigger others."

I nodded and grabbed a paper towel from the holder to wipe my eyes and blow my nose.

"That was very attractive," Carver said. "I can see why Jack loves you."

A laugh burst out, surprising me. "And you were doing so well. Almost human."

"Don't tell anyone," he said. "Now that I've softened you up, I can tell you the real reason I'm here."

"Jesus, there's more? Maybe I should've gotten the vodka down instead of the cake."

"As long as you're not doing surgery on

anyone, I'm okay with that. I started looking through the flash drives you gave me that belonged to your father."

He said it quickly, laying out the facts as precisely as possible, and I felt my blood run cold.

"First of all, I've never encountered the level of security to gain access to those flash drives. They're set to erase if I make a wrong move, and it's a painstaking process that I still haven't broken through. But I've managed to get past the outer walls, and I'm going to tell you right now, because I'm your friend, if you want me to stop I will. I'll give them back and I can develop amnesia about the whole thing."

I closed my eyes, trying to decide which pain I should feel today. Between Jack and my father, I was running on emotional fumes. Even though I'd resigned myself to my father's actions some time ago, I still felt the sting. As much as I wanted to, I couldn't harden myself completely.

"It's bad?" I asked.

"From what I've seen so far, it could be really bad." He sighed and went to refill his cup. "I know he's alive. I've uncovered that much. Your determination wouldn't be so strong if he wasn't. And the contents of a dead man's flash drives wouldn't be nearly so important."

"I want you to keep going. I don't know what my dad is capable of. Not entirely. And if there's a chance that anyone else could be in danger, I can't live with that on my conscience."

"Yeah, that's what I thought you'd say."

I took the dishes to the sink and rinsed them out. "You've been a real ray of sunshine this trip, Carver. When are you going home?"

He laughed and I relaxed a little. Ben was a good guy. Strange. And I knew I was only seeing the surface—what he allowed me to see. Carver had secrets.

"You invited me to the rehearsal dinner tonight, and you promised me free cake at the wedding tomorrow. I'm not leaving until after that. I don't just leave my wife at home with the kids for nothing you know. Especially when the baby is teething."

"Thanks for coming, Ben. It means a lot to both of us."

"I saw the news coverage about Anthony Connelli and his family. Word is you ruled it a multiple homicide."

"A single injection of a paralytic to the neck in each victim. What do you think?"

"Sounds fishy. You might have a homicide

on your hands."

I rolled my eyes and then filled him in on the rest, leaving out the part where Jack and I may or may not be getting married the following day.

"Umm…hello, what am I? Chopped liver?" Ben patted his backpack lovingly. "I've got Matilda right here. I can have any information you need on the Bruces and anyone else in a matter of moments."

Matilda was Carver's computer. He'd built her from the ground up, and I had a feeling he babied her more than his own children.

"I don't think that's a good idea," I said, even though I kind of thought it was. "I don't want to interfere with Jack's investigation. And I don't want you to get in trouble. You've broken the law enough for us."

He pursed his lips, looking very prim all of a sudden. "I don't like to call it breaking the law. I like to call it circumventing the system. And if I ever get into trouble then I probably deserve the punishment, because if there's someone that works for the government in any capacity that's better at computers than I am, then I'll eat my hat. We're all on the side of the good guys. I'm a firm believer in getting justice however it needs to be accomplished."

"Jack's not like that," I said.

"No, Jack's not like that. He deserves to wear the white hat of a hero more than anyone I've ever known. He's a straight arrow. I have a white hat too, but I live in D.C. so it's gray with pollution and politicians' bullshit. But there's still a white hat under the dirt. You know what I'm saying?"

"That your wife deserves sainthood?" I asked, arching a brow.

"No doubt about that. Now let me get Matilda out of the bag and see what she can do. She's been cooped up all morning, and I've got nothing else to do in this town except watch that old lady park on the median. Your wedding has an open bar, right?"

"I have no idea. I'm just supposed to show up. You know the relationship you have with your computer is not natural, don't you?"

"You're not the first person to tell me that. But I'm secure in my masculinity. I mean, look at me. I'm pretty awesome."

"Fine, but if Jack gets mad, you have to take the blame. I'm supposed to get married this weekend, dammit."

CHAPTER THIRTEEN

"Let's start with financials," Ben said. "That's usually where all the good stuff is."

"It depends on whose financials you're looking at. Mine aren't all that exciting."

I stood over Ben's shoulder and watched his fingers fly across the keyboard. He'd mumble under his breath every once in a while and then he'd give Matilda an encouraging word or two.

"It looks like John and Cherise have three joint accounts out of First National in D.C. Not surprising all of them have healthy amounts. One looks like their regular household account to pay bills and tuition for both children," he said, scrolling down on the screen. "The other two are savings accounts. Both are in the seven figures and no withdrawals have been made lately, but regular deposits are made monthly.

"Cherise has a checking account just in her name. It looks like she has a healthy shoe habit, regular spa visits, and twice weekly tennis lessons. What she pays in country club fees equals my yearly salary. Let's go back further and see if there are any other patterns."

"Everything looks the same," I said a couple of minutes later. "She's the most boring woman on the face of the planet."

"Let's check the Senator. Maybe he's a little less boring."

A few minutes later we had our answer. "Even his campaign contributions are on the up and up from what I can tell," Carver said. "It's just not right. No extra kickbacks. No bribes that I can find. What kind of politician is this guy?"

"A good one apparently. Maybe you should vote on him in the next election."

"It's like he's offered me a direct challenge to dig up some dirt. Okay, Senator. I accept your challenge. Let's see what your personal computers look like."

"You can just tap into his personal

computers?"

"Sure. The problem with modern technology is everything is backed up through a mobile system. Once it's in the air like that, it's anyone's for the taking if they know what the hell they're doing. Which is mostly me and a bunch of fourteen and fifteen year old hackers who I'm going to try to recruit for the side of good in the next decade or so."

"Emails to and from his kids and to other senators. A very busy calendar. A reminder to book reservations for his anniversary. Booooring. There's not even any porn in his browser history or record of a parking ticket. What kind of man has never had a parking ticket in Washington, D.C.? It's not normal."

"You should be glad your representative is on the up and up."

"I personally think it's a little disappointing. I have expectations of today's government officials and I expect them to be upheld."

"You work for the government, Carver."

"Which is exactly why I have the expectations to begin with. Matilda, darling. Let's see if we can dig deeper and see what the Senate Defense Committee is working on of late. That's going to take a little time, so who else are players in this mess?"

"Doctor Lance Owens. Jack said he's

scheduled to come in to the station for interview this morning. He performed the plastic surgery on Julia Connelli and erased it from her medical files."

I noticed my cup was empty and resisted the temptation to get another refill. Instead, I went to the fridge and grabbed a bottle of water.

"What if Senator Bruce is so good he's bad," I said, thought popping into my head.

"I have no idea what that means."

"I mean say Bruce is as good as he seems on paper. He's a straight arrow. And all of a sudden he finds out his best friend's wife has faked her entire existence and is taking payments from the Russian government to keep them informed on what her husband is working on."

"Ahh, I see where you're going with it. He'd be pissed, especially if Anthony Connelli is tied to anything the Defense Committee has going at the moment."

"But would he kill his best friend just to get to the wife? And the children too? If he's a good as it seems he is that would be out of character. Because whoever administered those shots knew every one in that household would die once the fire started. That kind of preparation is pre-meditated murder."

Carver shrugged. "Then you get back to the argument of the death of a few versus the death of many. I guess it would just depend on what kind of sensitive material she had her hands on. If any. Maybe Julia was the target all along. What if the Russians deposited that money in her account and she didn't deliver on the job? Maybe she really loved her children and husband and ignored her orders. As smoothly as the murder happened, from the injections to the way the fire was started, it could have been a professional job all along. Someone hired by the Russian government. And if that's the case, the chances of finding the killer aren't all that great. He's probably already back home by now."

"That's a comforting thought. But you make a good point. Other than that three million dollar deposit the week before the murders, were any others made?"

"I'll look. I printed out the information on Lance Owens, as well as the wife."

I let Carver do his computer thing and went back to my office where I had the wireless printer hooked up. Papers were still coming out so I checked my text messages while I waited. Still nothing from Jack. That wasn't a good sign. Even when we were working we had the tendency to check in with each other throughout the day.

I put my phone back in my pocket and gathered the papers, looking through the financials of the Owens and their backgrounds. It was information the police already had, but I hadn't had a chance to look through them at the house that morning. I was especially interested in Doctor Owens' records as a surgeon. He'd had a few malpractice lawsuits, but that wasn't uncommon. And he had less than most would with the number of years he'd been practicing.

I walked back into the kitchen and Carver said, "No other deposits made before the one last week. Which certainly lends credence to her ignoring their wishes. She's been in the states a long time. Her husband has powerful friends and has his own power in certain circles. Maybe she didn't realize the lengths they'd go to if she ignored them. The Connellis had the original issues with Wayne Macerne, so I was thinking he'd be the most likely suspect. But now I'm not so sure."

"You find anything interesting about the Owens?" he asked. "Also, would you grab me a bottle of water? I know better than to drink coffee. I get all jittery. I'm going to have energy all day, girl. I hope there's dancing tonight at the rehearsal dinner. The single ladies love it when I dance."

"They also probably love the wedding ring on your finger."

"You think I should take it off?"

"Only if you want your wife to kill you."

"Good point. She's mean. If she was going to kill me, she'd make it hurt."

"If you're going to do something, do it right, I always say." I spread the printed papers on the Owens out on the kitchen island. "Nothing unusual in his professional files. He's got a great reputation and his client list never leaks, so it's rumored that he's the official plastic surgeon of the stars. He makes a very comfortable eight figures a year. He also has Ehlers-Danlos Syndrome."

"I don't know what that is, but anything with the word syndrome at the end is never good."

"It's a hereditary disease where the connective tissue in the body is weakened. So all the joints are very flexible and it's easy for them to slip out of socket. It also weakens the connective tissue of the skin, so the skin stretches more than it would for a normal person. When I met Owens for the first time I was surprised by his appearance, considering his age. His face was deeply wrinkled and sagged in places, but now it makes sense.

"I wondered why he hadn't gotten plastic surgery to take care of it. You'd think appearances would be extremely important to someone in that field, but now I realize he didn't have surgery because he couldn't. With the elasticity and fragility of the skin, it won't hold stitches. The skin stretches around them and has a tendency to tear."

"You said it was hereditary," Carver said. "Did his daughter have it?"

"No, and I would have found it when I did the autopsy."

"Anything new on Mrs. Owens? Other than wowza. That woman is beautiful."

"She's also old enough to be your mother."

"I'm alright with cougars. They know things."

"I'm not even going to ask how you know that."

"My senior year of college I dated a girl finishing up her PhD in English. It was—" he paused and pinched his fingers and thumb together, bringing it to his lips and kissing them in an Italian gesture—"magic."

"Whatever happened to her?"

"She's at home with a teething baby."

CHAPTER FOURTEEN

At ten o'clock I oversaw the transfer of Cassandra Owens to a funeral home in D.C. Once I signed off on the paperwork, I went by the cemetery to make sure everything was going right with Bernie Harrison's gravesite funeral service.

I'm not sure what had me driving back by the house, but with the new setup I was thinking that's where the team probably was. I was surprised to find only Jack's cruiser in the driveway. And I was ashamed to say I almost turned around and went back into town rather than face him.

My hand paused over the doorknob and I finally turned it and pushed it open. Jack was in the front room where I'd left him, studying one of the white boards. It had been filled in more since I'd left. I stood at the door and watched him, the breadth of his shoulders as he stood with hands on hips and looked at the board with rapt concentration. Don't get me wrong, he knew I was there, but he wasn't sure how to handle the situation any better than I did.

"I heard you talked to Carver," he finally said. He still didn't turn around, but I was grateful he'd at least broken the silence.

"I'd like to say it was all his idea. I told him I didn't want to interfere in your investigation."

He turned his body slightly so he could see me and arched a brow. "I'm talking about what he said as far as my PTSD goes. What are you talking about?"

"Umm…never mind," I said, clearing my throat. "Don't be angry with Ben. He didn't tell me anything specific. Even though I recognized it for what it was once I got some space between us and had time to calm down and think things through. I should have recognized it in you before. I know the signs. Have seen it up close and personal while I was working at the hospital. But you shouldn't have waited for me to recognize it. You should have trusted me enough to tell me how bad it can get."

He dropped down into one of the chairs and put his head in his hands. Then he scrubbed at his face and I saw the tears in his eyes. My heart broke to see him hurting and every ounce of anger and frustration I'd been feeling drained from my body. I kneeled down in front of him and rested my head on his knee, comforting as best I could. I didn't ask any questions, but waited on him to tell me as much as he needed to.

He cleared his throat once—and then again—and said, "It doesn't happen often. Usually if I let stress build or if something happens it'll trigger a response. And the last couple of weeks, when I had to watch men I'd commanded die and remember the nightmare of that last raid in D.C., it was like reliving it all again. The overwhelming grief and the helplessness I felt to do something to save them, and my failure to do so."

His fingers touched the ends of my hair and his other hand twined with mine. I should have realized what an effect the last case we worked would have had on Jack. I knew it had been hard on him, but I hadn't understood to what lengths. Jack took the responsibility of command seriously, and for his men to die because of something he'd had no control over years before was a bitter pill to swallow.

"The depression gets overwhelming. Like I said, it doesn't affect me often, but when it does it's like a weight pressing against my chest. There are some days I don't want to even get out of bed."

I brought my head up so I could look him in the eye, trying to decide if I'd been that callous in not noticing or if he'd been that good at hiding it from me.

"This is the first time it's happened since you and I became involved. I think, in a way, you being next to me at night somehow kept it all at bay. I was relieved, to tell you the truth. I'd been worried I'd wake you up in the middle of the night, my body drenched in sweat and the nightmares still on the tip of my tongue. You somehow brought balance to the horrors I've seen and done in this life."

"But not this time," I said, trying to understand what I could do to keep the balance in the future. Or at least ease the burden.

"It's nothing you did or could have done. There will be days that are harder than others. And on the days that it's a struggle for me to get out of bed, nothing but my own stubbornness puts my feet on the floor and gets me moving. I hate being weak—

especially in front of you—but I know I can trust you to see that side of me and not judge or feel sorry for me."

"I won't feel sorry for you, but I'll hurt for you because I love you. All you ever have to do is talk to me. I'll never demand anything from you that you can't give."

"I love you," he said, resting his forehead against mine. "And I'm sorry for this morning. I don't have any excuse for talking to you that way or not talking to you when it starts to affect me. It's going to take some adjustment on my part, so I ask that you be patient with me. I've never, and I mean never, told anyone about this. Not my parents, a counselor, or a priest. I'm used to keeping everything inside, so my first reaction is going to be to hide it from you. But I promise I will do my best."

"You always give me your best," I said.

"Have I told you how glad I am that you're going to be my wife?"

"It's been a few days. So I'm really glad to hear that I didn't try on that dress for nothing yesterday."

"Now that we've got that out of the way, maybe we can go back to what you were saying about Carver opening his big mouth before."

"I don't remember saying anything about Carver's big mouth. Or Matilda's."

Jack arched his eyebrow. "I should've known he'd have butted his nose in regardless. Carver likes playing Robin Hood. You might as well tell me what you found out."

I got to my feet and held out my hand to Jack. He took it and stood with me, holding my hand loosely as we walked back to the board and I filled him in on everything Ben was able to find. Which really wasn't all that much. It was looking like Jack was right. This case might not get solved at all, much less before our wedding.

"What about Lance Owens? Did he come in to meet with Lewis and Martinez?"

"He had to call and reschedule. Said he was needed at the hospital."

"Look on the bright side. In a few hours we'll be eating delicious food with your family and our closest friends." I'd never been so grateful that I didn't have any remaining family. I couldn't imagine the stress of having them there on top of the stress of getting married in general. "If we're really lucky someone will get drunk and entertain the masses all night and we can sneak away early."

"You're always thinking, Graves."

CHAPTER FIFTEEN

Jack and I spent most of the rest of the afternoon studying the data we'd collected on anyone involved with the Connelli family, with the exception of when I had to leave at three o'clock to oversee the transfer of their remains to Robert Connelli, Anthony's brother.

The problem with data was there was a lot to process, and sometimes the best thing was to let it soak into the brain and rattle around in there awhile. Then sometimes things started making some sense.

I'd resigned myself to the fact that the information was just going to have to rattle until we got back from our honeymoon. I'd avoided Vaughn's texts all day, asking whether or not I'd kept the appointments for a manicure and pedicure, and whether or not I'd carved out the time to let someone else trim my hair besides me.

I mentally stuck my tongue out at the phone every time it dinged with another one of Vaughn's messages, and finally he got the hint and didn't send anything else after he told me it was fine with him if I wanted to have troll feet at my wedding. I personally didn't think my feet looked troll like, but just in case I was grateful my shoes had closed toes.

The problem with all the information rattling in my brain was that subconsciously I knew the answer was there. The problem was sifting through all the bullshit before I found what I was looking for. I just had a weird feeling about the whole thing. Like maybe we were making things too complicated.

I'd somehow found myself dressed in a lavender sheath dress, stockings, and dark purple heels. Vaughn had picked everything out, so I knew I didn't look like an idiot. Even though I felt like one. And I'd even managed to find the time to have Roberta Cleary trim my hair when she came by the funeral parlor to touch up Chloe Anderson's hair and makeup.

Jack came downstairs dressed in a dark suit

and tie and I just stared in appreciation. I was one lucky woman.

"How much time do we have before the thing starts?" I asked.

"We're supposed to meet at the church in an hour and do a quick rehearsal of what's going to happen tomorrow, and then we're supposed to have dinner at the country club after that. They've got a private room set up for us there. Why?"

"Do we have time to run an errand?"

"Depends on the errand. Are you wanting to go to Vegas again?"

"Also, why do we have to rehearse what's going to happen tomorrow? It makes no sense. If we're doing it tonight we might as well get married tonight. Why do it twice?"

"Strangely enough, I agree with you completely about this one. I don't get it either. But it will make my mother and Vaughn happy so we're wearing our fancy clothes and are going to show up. Now what's the errand?"

I shrugged and grabbed the matching sweater that came with the dress in case it turned cool that evening.

"Do we have time to pay a visit to Kelsey Donaldson? There's just something weird about that whole thing."

"Like what?"

"The timeline. Michael Bruce said he left the Connellis around six o'clock. And Kelsey works in D.C. and said Michael was waiting for her there at the hotel after she got off work. She said she was there before seven, but she didn't get off work until six o'clock. It takes more than an hour to get from D.C. to Fredericksburg. And this would have been Tuesday night. You remember what happened in D.C. on Tuesday night?"

Jack thought for a second and then it came to him. "The union protestors," he said. "The police had to block off six square blocks around the capitol building because of the number of people who showed up. If Kelsey works at a restaurant by the capitol building she would've been stuck there for a while. The news said traffic was at a standstill for almost two hours while commuters tried to get home from work and avoid the protestors all at the same time. Yeah, I think we have time to pay Kelsey Donaldson a visit."

Carver came bounding down the stairs about that time dressed in a navy suit and a Star Wars tie.

"Did I just hear you say you were going somewhere besides your wedding rehearsal?" he asked, looking back and forth between us expectantly. "Because I could be wrong, but I think it's a requirement for the bride and groom to be at shit for their wedding."

Jack explained about the timeline discrepancies with Kelsey's story and Ben nodded in agreement. "If we leave now, we can be back by dinnertime and you only have to miss the rehearsal part. I don't see the point of the wedding rehearsal anyway. Why not just get married if you're going to the trouble to walk down the aisle and say your vows anyway?"

"I never thought of it that way, Carver," Jack said, straight-faced. "If anyone asks, we'll tell them this was your idea."

The closer we got to Kelsey Donaldson's house, where she lived with her aunt, the more my gut churned, telling me I was missing something important. I looked through Kelsey's file again, and read the transcript of her interview with Lewis.

Jack got on the phone and called his mother, letting her know to go ahead and go through the rehearsal without us and to give people plenty of wine so they don't notice we're not there.

"I feel a little like a third wheel," Carver said from the back seat of Jack's truck. Since we were all dressed up, we decided it probably wasn't the best thing to take Jack's unit and put Carver in the back seat like a criminal.

"Going to talk to someone related to a murder investigation isn't a normal date night for us, you weirdo," Jack said.

"Hey, how am I supposed to know that? It seems like something you two might do. Y'all are the weirdos."

By the time we pulled up at the little house Kelsey shared with her aunt, my Spidey senses were tingling. Jack and Ben's must have been too because Jack reached under his seat and pulled out a backup weapon and tucked it in at the small of his back.

It was a small box of a house, dingy white with peeling paint and a sagging porch. I was feeling rather naked without being able to wear my own weapon. It was tucked in my handbag, but I'd gotten into the habit of having it on my body at all times.

"I'll slide around to the back door," Carver said. "Just in case."

Jack nodded and we waited until Carver started around the side of the house before we got out and made our way to the front door. We'd just rung the doorbell when

Carver came back around the side of the house.

"Nobody's going to be answering that door today," Carver said. "I can see a DB through the window."

Jack called the Chief of Police in Fredericksburg, who was a friend of his, since this wasn't our jurisdiction and we didn't have the right to enter the house or examine the dead body. Or bodies. Once the first responders came they ended up finding the body of an older woman—my guess was the aunt—in one of the bedrooms. Both she and Kelsey had been shot at close range.

"We're just going back to the wedding rehearsal?" I asked.

"Be thankful you were able to get out of the rehearsal part," Jack said. "But we shouldn't push it about missing the dinner. It's not a good idea to cross my mother. Besides, there's nothing we can do there except wait to get a report from the investigating officer. It's not my city and those aren't my bodies. He said he'd send over initial findings as soon as he could. Which will be Monday at the earliest. And we'll be gone anyway."

"We need to find Michael Bruce. I called my old boss in D.C. and they're going to send someone to do drive-bys to see if they can spot him."

"But what's his motivation?" I asked. "He's a kid that's got everything in the world at his fingertips. His parents seem to be good people. Why would he kill five people?"

"We won't know until we talk to him. But he's found himself in a position of not having two best friends. His friends are now a couple and he's the odd man out. By all accounts, there's some rivalry between him and Damian Connelli at school as far as their class rank. And now all of a sudden he's the first in his class. It could be something as simple as that. We need to find him and talk to him."

"The Bruces are going to put up roadblocks," I said.

"Yep."

"Ben, can you do an in depth search on Michael Bruce?"

"Umm...of course I can. I'm brilliant and amazing at my job. No one's secrets are safe from me."

"A disturbing thought," I said.

"I thought you already read through his file," Jack asked.

"I read through the one you guys did at the house. He's got a ridiculous trust fund, but other than that there was no information other than school records and his community service history. I want to see if Carver can find something deeper."

"The kid's only seventeen," Jack said. "I don't know how much deeper you can go."

Ben set up some kind of remote wireless system in the back seat of the truck and got out Matilda.

"You really do take her everywhere," I said. "It's a little creepy."

"Don't judge what you don't understand, Graves. You'd want me to leave her at home by herself when everyone is going to be out having a good time tonight? That's just cruel."

We were silent a few minutes while Carver worked and then he finally said, "Nope, Jack's right. This is a seventeen year old kid. He doesn't have much of a secret life. At least not that I can find, which means it doesn't exist cause I can find anything."

"The ego—"

"I like to call it confidence." Carver scrolled through some more information. "But listen, there's nothing here. The most exciting thing that's happened to this kid when he broke his arm a couple of years ago. Bone broke through the skin and they couldn't get it to heal right. They ended up testing him for cancer, but the scans came back negative."

"And there it is—" I said as the tumblers in my mind all fell into place. "Jack, you remember when we were talking to the Bruces and they mentioned the paper cut on his finger that was still bleeding through the Band-Aid?"

"Yeah, because he went out dirt biking. I got the impression that he had some kind of disease."

"Yeah, I bet you a million dollars he's got Ehlers-Danlos Syndrome and it's never been diagnosed. It's often overlooked when people show the symptoms with skin first and not their joints."

"You said that was hereditary," Carver said.

"It is. And I bet you double or nothing that Lance Owens is Michael Bruce's real father. The odds of them both having the disease without sharing blood would astronomical."

"I wonder if Michael knew Lance Owens was his father," Jack said.

"If he did, he might be pretty pissed. Though I'm not sure why the Connellis would be his target."

"Maybe the Connellis weren't his target. Maybe the girl was all along."

Jack called into the station and asked for officers to be dispatched to pick up both

Michael Bruce and Lance Owens. "Lewis and Martinez can deal with it tonight. Actually, they're going to have to wrap up the whole thing. We have things to do."

We'd just passed the sign on the road letting us know we'd entered King George County when a black SUV came out of nowhere and rammed us from behind. My head jerked and hit the side of the window hard enough that I saw stars. Whoever hit us hit exactly at the right angle on the bed of the truck to send us into a spin.

Jack was a good driver and was able to minimize the damage, but there was only so much he could do. The airbags deployed and I jerked against the seatbelt, and then the truck tilted and we went face first into a culvert.

I sat slumped against my seatbelt, my mind not caught up with what had just happened. I was stunned, but my medical training kicked in and I started cataloging the different aches and pains through my body to see if any of them were serious.

A different kind of training kicked in for Jack. By the time I was able to lift my head, he'd cut through his seatbelt and was out of the car, drawing his weapon. Two shots were fired and I held my breath until I realized they were from Jack's weapon and not someone shooting at us.

I was pretty much trapped in the truck since we'd hit the culvert on my side, and I couldn't get the door open. I struggled with my seatbelt and pushed myself up so I could see out of Jack's door to the street. The SUV that had hit us had swerved out of control and Jack had shot out the tires before the culprit could drive away.

"Get out of the car slowly. Hands up and away from your body," Jack said.

My muscles trembled as I held myself up, and I was losing strength. My vision was starting to go blurry and I was pretty sure I had a concussion after my head made contact with the window. I saw he had everything under control and dropped back into the seat.

"Get your hands up and get on the ground," I heard him say.

I looked back at Carver and saw he was knocked out cold. Matilda was a mess of pieces across the seat and floorboard. I unbuckled my own seatbelt so I could turn around and I put two fingers against the pulse in his neck. And then I opened up his lids to check his pupils. I didn't see any external bleeding, but that didn't mean he didn't have internal issues.

I called 911 and talked to Kendra in

dispatch to request an ambulance and backup officers. Almost as soon as I made the request, I heard the sirens blaring. I could feel the blackness closing in on me. I shook off the blackness that kept encroaching, not wanting to leave Jack alone until backup arrived.

I heard the sirens get closer and car doors slam, but I couldn't stay awake any longer. The blackness came whether I wanted it to or not.

I'd regained consciousness by the time they loaded me in the ambulance to take me to the hospital. Jack rode beside me, and he looked a bit like a pirate with a bandage wrapped around his head and blood dripping from the corner of his eye.

What they say about doctors making the worst patients is true. We weren't halfway to the hospital by the time I was asking them to take out the IV and let me go.

"I'm still getting married in the morning, Jack Lawson. Don't you dare try to make me stay in the hospital. I'm fine. I just got my brains scrambled a little. I'll have a headache and we'll both be very colorful tomorrow if my aches and pains are anything to show for it, but I am walking down that aisle no matter what."

His teeth flashed white and he winced as it opened the cut near his eye again. "I wouldn't let you miss it for the world."

"Was it Michael Bruce?" I asked.

Jack nodded. "It's a damned shame. He's a bright kid. But he's been sheltered his whole life in this perfect world created for him, and then all of a sudden he finds out it's a lie. He'd confessed to everything by the time they got you and Carver out of the car.

"It turns out he and Cassie are the ones who had a thing going for a little while. And then he found out about his mother's affair with Lance Owens and when he confronted her about it she told him the truth. But by the time he knew Cassie was his half sister, the damage was done. He broke things off with her and the only explanation he gave was that he liked it when they were all just friends better. She was obviously hurt, but her reaction was to move onto Damian Connelli as kind of a big middle finger."

"That's a really big middle finger," I said, wincing.

"Yep, and he was really pissed. I told you his IQ was off the charts. And a sociopath with a high IQ is always a dangerous thing, even at a young age. But he's got a bit of a temper and that's his weakness. If he'd have laid low and not overreacted when he saw us going back to talk to Kelsey he might have gotten away with it. He'd set up Lance Owens to take the fall pretty convincingly.

"We would have found the drug you found in the Connelli's system missing from the hospital with his signature on the line. And I guarantee the blood Walker found on the coffee pot would've belonged to Owens too."

"Creepy kid," I said, shuddering. My body was coming out of shock and I couldn't keep myself from shaking, so I just let it run its course. "I hate to break it to you, but I'm going to be out again here in a second or two. Just make sure you wake me up for the wedding."

"Will do, Doctor Graves." He brought my hand to his lips and kissed my fingers, and that was the last thing I remembered before sliding into sleep.

EPILOGUE

There are those snapshots in time—the ones that are imprinted in the mind forever—when everything becomes slow motion and in focus so you can see every particle of the moment being captured.

Today was that moment for me.

I wouldn't necessarily remember every detail of my dress, the cake, or the faces in the crowd when I was ninety years old and playing the memories of my youth on a loop through my mind. If I had to forget anything it would be the aches in my body and the bruises that covered my torso, but even those were their own memory—another story of our life to tell.

I might not remember details about myself,

but I'd remember everything about Jack. The way the setting sun haloed around him, casting a golden glow across everything it touched, and the black eye and stitches along the outside of his eye. God, we looked like a pair and my lips twitched as I had the thought.

But it was the look of complete and utter awe on his face as I walked toward him—the love there so radiant and pure that I wondered how anyone could miss it—that made me forget the aches and pains.

I knew family and friends surrounded us, but for that snapshot in time it was only me and Jack. It had always been the two of us. It was a little strange to think of myself as someone's wife—Jack's wife—but that's what I wanted to be.

And as I met Jack beneath an arch of white flowers and took his hand, I made those vows, and promised to love, honor, and cherish him until death did us part. For once the thought of death didn't weigh heavy on my heart, because in that moment, so filled with the promise of our love to each other, I knew that not even death could separate us.

ABOUT THE AUTHOR

Liliana Hart is the New York Times and USA Today bestselling author of more than a thirty books. She lives in Texas in a big rambling house with her laptop and cats, and she spends way too much time on Twitter. She loves hearing from her readers.

Made in the USA
Columbia, SC
16 May 2020

97575996R00124